Offer in the Flat

Q. T. Porta

Grosvenor House
Publishing Limited

This book is published by
Grosvenor House Publishing Ltd
Link House
140 The Broadway, Tolworth, Surrey, KT6 7HT.
www.grosvenorhousepublishing.co.uk

This novel's story and characters are fictitious. Certain long-standing
institutions, events, and public offices are mentioned, but the
characters involved are imaginary. Any resemblance to actual persons,
living or dead is purely coincidental.

A CIP record for this book
is available from the British Library

ISBN 978-1-83615-231-6

Acknowledgements

I watch the years passing at an increased pace and think of how different our lives would be if we took the time to pause and ponder. Do we miss chances, or do we push them away?

In retrospect, my family have given support, surprises, and strife, however it would have been impossible to finish the novel without their empathy and encouragement.

The temptation is to only thank each person who offered kindness, but there is recognition for those who misused their senior role, because they inadvertently opened the door to new opportunities. They had a part to play but will not partake in the future chapters of my life.

The guidance and help from Grosvenor House Publishing Ltd is invaluable. I enjoyed writing essays in school and dreamed of writing a novel. I remained hopeful, with a few blips, for the next five decades and with unrelentless joy can now say – "I am an author."

And last but by no means least, I thank you – the reader: for your generosity to buy the book, for your support and for each time you encourage others to share in the wonderment of reading.

I congratulate all independent bookshops who strive to remain open and contribute to a thriving High Street – a vital part of a strong community.

Q. T. Porta
2025

CHAPTER 1

The crumbled edges of the card squashed through the torn side of the envelope.

'*No need to worry,*' I thought. '*The card will not be used this year nor ever again. However, I am not going to the shop to ask for a refund.*'

Cards are bought in advance, in hope, but gather dust and deteriorate in the aftermath of loss. When the grip of grief eases and strength is restored, the remnants are moved to a different place and steps are taken towards the new stage.

My dad passed away on Friday 9th December 2022.

I am clinging onto my Father's Day card.

***

Joanna Tabitha Crowmere–Gale, my niece, is feisty, fearless, and fun, with a smattering of fragility hidden behind her shield. She hates her name with a vengeance so shortens it to Jo except on legal documents e.g. job applications. Her father selected the names – not a matter of levity but control. Joanna is a feminine version of Jonathan, one of his middle names, and Tabitha is in honour of his mother.

My niece insisted we meet in central London in attempt to cover over the cracks of a Father's Day without a father. She had an absent father during her childhood–he left the family home when she was five years old. Her stepfather is not even on her radar, and her granddad bid a final farewell six months ago. We are all reeling from the aftershock and coping in our inherent ways. I would really like to curl up with a good book, such as, *A Week in Winter* by Maeve Binchy: a work of art – the words are perfectly painted into a framework of an exquisite song of simplicity which is far from simple once you see the intricacy of the fine stitches sewn together, to make a patchwork quilt which wraps securely around your shoulders.

Shaftesbury Avenue thrived on the noise and joviality amidst the celebrations of Father's Day on Sunday, 18th June 2023. Restaurants, bars, and the pavements were full. The hustle and bustle recharged the energy of the crowd buzzing around like busy bees in a hive, whereas I find it draining, but did not want to leave my niece to face another Father's Day on her own.

"I was going to bring you backstage, but the Director didn't want any disturbances today after last night's performance or should I say lack of performance. He's not in any mood for hospitality!" My niece made the announcement with the sound of exhaustion lingering on her lips.

"Can I ask what happened?" The intention of my question was light-hearted interest but was not interpreted in the same spirit.

"NO!" came the sharp note – a semitone higher than the usual riposte. "Cosimo is under a mountain of pressure and doesn't want a leak on socials. He would go ballistic – I just about calmed him down last night. He is not sleeping well."

"Really?" I enquired with a smirk that irritates my niece to the umpteenth degree. "Is that your new crush?"

"Stop trying to be funny Aunty," she bit back. "Never works and the Comedy Club is closed. Even if it was open, you wouldn't get in. So can we have a serious conversation like adults."

"Yes, of course," I replied. "But seriously; I don't know how to set up socials never mind spill the beans."

"No good trying to be satirical," Jo responded, "that's worse than your so-called jokes."

I thought it was it best to call a halt to teasing my niece because her neck was turning a tone of raging red matching her cheeks. She works hard: a more accurate description – hides at work. Her father bought a studio flat for her convenience, in Upper Berkeley Street, W1H; an eleven-minute bicycle ride to theatre land. Her mother and me, in fact the entire family, worry about the bicycle option however she insists she does not want to get entangled with the squashed sardines a.k.a. commuters, on the underground. I entirely agree with her sentiment and am baffled how we surrender to squeeze into ever smaller available spaces on public transport and pay ever increasing fares. A conundrum for the modern age. When the roads are layered with ice or protestors, the walking option only takes about thirty minutes on her speedy feet. My best time is approximately forty-five minutes with my speedy boots on. Thank goodness for my old, wide fitting, storm-grip rubber outsole, cushion insole, and waterproof, walking shoes. Not a fashion statement, but my ankles cannot tackle the obstacles when trying to get on and off trains without support. In a culture filled to the brim with health and safety regulations, could anyone design a mini bridge to reduce the daunting gap between the train and the edge of the platform?

The stifling heat prompted my niece to make a suggestion, which came across as a stage instruction from the director of a play. "You can drop off your bag at my flat followed by a quick freshen up." I don't drop my bag off anywhere and she is only too aware of how my rucksack is attached to me (not literally!) She looked tired and her eyes were filled with melancholy, but the stubbornness stood in the way of seeking help.

"My feet would appreciate a rest, and a cup of tea would be wonderful." I replied.

"Rock 'n' Roll lifestyle!" She said sarcastically.

"Just R&R will be fine," I sighed with relief.

The dishevelled duvet and the spoon stuck to the unwashed cereal bowl on the floor, by the grey corduroy, refillable, classic bean bag, signalled the need for a helping hand.

"No milk left," she proclaimed from inside the small fridge. "Do you want a green tea?"

I slumped on the sofa bed which was much lower than I had anticipated. "Oh my!" I gasped as I rolled over onto my side. "Sorry! No that's okay. Do you have a cold drink?"

"Fizzy black current juice? Is that alright?"

I was not sure what 'fizzy' meant in this context but accepted the offer with an additional request, "are there any ice cubes?"

"No," came the disgruntled reply. "Freezer drawer stopped working yesterday. "

"That's fine," I said whilst taking one of the old theatre brochures from the pile on the coffee table to wave in front of my face in a futile effort to replicate a domestic air conditioning unit. It was not a good understudy.

"Why are you laying down?" Jo asked abruptly. "We're not staying long."

"I'm not laying down; I can't get up!" My pitiful reply prompted my niece to laugh loudly. Nice to see a spark on her face albeit briefly.

"How old are you?" She mocked. "Have you signed up for the Pilates classes yet?"

"It's on my to do list," I replied defensively. "And, you know my age – I am 60."

"That old!" She smirked. "Sorry, forgot to post your card. Anyway, snail mail takes too long."

"My birthday was in May!" I exclaimed. "I know there are delays with the post but it's not that bad. I am sure you were thinking of me?"

"Of course. Always thinking of my favourite old Aunty!" She said accompanied by a cheeky smile.

"I know my favourite niece thinks of me every hour of every day, especially when she wants something."

"I'm your only niece!" She protested.

The dusty blinds let in shards of sun light onto the compact, cluttered, and cosmopolitan accommodation. I tipped my toes into the shark filled water expecting to be bitten but wanted to search the depth of the shadow underneath the surface.

"Did you send your dad a card?"

"WHY?" she snapped.

"Hate to state the obvious, but he's your dad." I replied softly with a mild reproof.

"Was my dad," she shrieked. "He's dead to me!" Joanna saw the searing pain slap me in the face (metaphorically speaking) and stopped. "Sorry. My foot slips off the brake pedal at times."

"Foot slips into your mouth, at times." I retorted.

My niece smiled – she enjoyed the banter and confidently knew I ran out of material before she even got started. "Do you miss granddad?" she asked with a sensitivity that she hides most of the time.

"Yes," I mumbled. "Always will. I was a daddy's girl. Baby Bunting or Baby Bumbling more like. But I am a big girl now and need to get on."

"Mum says you should go and move near her. Why not? What's your latest excuse? Go on Aunty, please share, will be fun!"

I took a sip of the chilled blackcurrant juice mixed with sparkling mineral water before replying, "if you've got the mystical magic fairy wand, I'll click my heels and can whizz off to a new home with new furniture, clothes and super-fast broadband!"

"You definitely need new shoes – those worn-out things are not in The Wizard of Oz"? She cackled. The impersonation of a fictional witch was quite unnerving.

"Thank you for your fashion tips," I said. "Just be grateful you have not inherited the elephant feet."

Jo looked bemused. "Mum hasn't got big feet?"

"I know. I know," I acknowledged wearily. "Can we change the subject please? Have you heard from Aldo?"

"Who?" My niece snapped defensively.

"Don't play Miss Innocent," I replied, "you are a good actor, but you need to rehearse that line a few more times!"

"You sound like the theatre critics – commentating on something you don't understand." Jo pouted as she delivered the rebuttal.

I nodded in recognition of her reaction, "okay. Firm but fair. I assume you will not be in contact with Aldo again?"

"Maybe?" Jo replied whilst developing a distance emotionally.

"Elusive like a butterfly." I wondered what she was hiding. "Anyone new on the scene?"

My niece lashed out when in a corner. "We are not on Mastermind; was tempted to say University Challenge but you didn't make it to university."

"We have so much in common!" I replied, sighed, and paused to allow the sting to be released from the atmosphere.

I tried a different approach. "It is too hot to argue, and ice-cream takes priority, right at this moment. We can go to Barnadi's? I could stretch to a pizza and cocktail."

"I wish!" Jo moaned. "Great there, and really yummy pizzas but it'll be jammed. Let's get an ice cream from Snowflake and sit in Hyde Park?"

"Do they sell fab ice lollies?" I asked mischievously.

"What?" my niece replied with indignation.

"You know," I said. "The one with 'hundreds and thousands' on the top. Dad used to buy one for me if I behaved when we went to the park. The ice-cream shop only opened for a little while, so I had to time it right. After I finished licking the lolly stick, I could run over to the big slide which made him nervous, especially after hitting my head during a Daddy Day Care outing. And the big roundabout: do you know it's called Witch's Hat? That was scary. Dad used to try to pull me off; he got a nasty bruise on his arm once, when the bully boys jumped on. I can still hear the clanging noise when it hit the metal pole in the middle. They laughed their heads off when I cried. I was banned from going to the park and from having *fab* ice-lollies for a month."

My niece rolled her eyes in exasperation and asked, "what are you goin' on about? I ain't got time to meander down memory lane. There's a large waffle with vanilla ice-cream with my name on it! Went there a couple of weeks ago for Chen's birthday." She blurted out the name without thinking – amidst the feeling of exhilaration generated by the entrance of a new boyfriend.

"Really! Do tell. Celebrating his 21st birthday again?" I probed and was taken aback by my niece's sudden coyness. "Please tell me he is over twenty-one?"

"Yes, of course," she retaliated. "I'm not a cougar. We're both young at heart and share the same interests and dreams."

"How young at heart?" I asked with trepidation.

"Twenty-five if you must know. Age is just a number. You're just jealous because you can't get a boyfriend." She knew how to hit the bullseye!

"Boyfriend? At my age? That ship has sailed long ago." I sighed but reluctantly accepted the reality that no one would find me physically attractive again. No more wolf whistles, not that those are allowed anymore and no more suggestive compliments about my appearance.

"Mum managed to snare a younger man and he's good looking. So why can't you follow in her footsteps?" my niece asked with a mixture of envy and spite.

"Stop being so catty, "I replied. "Come on then; tell me more, tell me more – like, does he have a car? Uh huh..."

My niece's raised voice drowned out my out of tune version of the superb song, Summer Nights, from the film Grease. "Stop right now!" She demanded.

"That's a Spice Girl's song, isn't it?" I teased my niece with a trivial question.

"You are so predictable!" she hit back with an anticipated outburst. "I'll tell you all about Chen; well, the edited version, in the park, after you have paid for my waffle."

***

My niece and me had a nice afternoon, on Father's Day, under the natural shade of the vintage trees in Hyde Park. Although surrounded by a mixture of noise, we created a personal space for a private conversation. Not surprisingly, the benches were full of rowdy tourists and worn-out mothers trying to persuade their toddlers to have one more spoonful of blended food, and older children to have one more cheese sandwich before having an ice-cream.

One rebellious toddler pressed his hands, covered in tomato sauce, against the side of the buggy, and stamped his feet on the frame resulting in his new trainers flying off his feet and hitting the pigeons who were eagerly waiting for a snack. The father stood at a distance whilst he finished his cigarette. The remarkable resemblance of the man and child re-affirmed my suspicions of the family connection. "Hold on to him for a minute!" The mother earnestly requested as she stretched out her arms towards her husband. "Sure, yeah. Just finish this." The nonchalant reply infuriated the mother. The football scores held his attention, and the latest likes on Facebook stole precious time with his child. Eventually the father took his son and over enthusiastically threw the toddler in the air. The squeals of joy and giggling rose above the hubbub in the park. The newly stained bib emblazoned with the statement, '*I dribble for Chelsea*' lifted to reveal the new blue tee-shirt with the words in bold white ink, 'I love my dad on Father's Day 2023. The back of the tee-shirt displayed the reassuring message: 'I love my dad every day.'

Jo cautiously described her relationship with Chen. She knows I share a generous portion of what she says with her mother therefore I am a useful free messaging service, or you could say 'piggy in the middle.' I am discreet when necessary: she sets out a caveat before informing me of life changing decisions i.e. "If you tell mum, I won't call you each week and won't get you free theatre tickets." At this juncture, I diplomatically point out she does not do neither so what exactly am I missing out on. You need to be able to bring something to the table before you negotiate a deal. After a lot of huffing and puffing and dispute about how many times she telephones me, we reach an agreement as to which circumstances will be conveyed directly to her mother. I know she knows my door is open if trouble strikes or the weight of her world is too heavy to carry albeit for a brief period.

The heady days of a new boyfriend may lead to a heavy heart. The foundation of her relationship with Chen does not sound solid and the fear is, they are both caught on the rebound. Her ex-boyfriend, not an accurate depiction: he is thirty years older than her. Nothing wrong with being sixty-five, but having been divorced three times, six children with his wives and three other children with mistresses was a cause for concern. Aldo Fabrizzi was born in Sicily in 1958 and moved to London in 1971 with his oldest brother to pursue his ambition to be an actor. My niece tolerated the teasing about the connection to the film, The Godfather, and blocked out the noise pollution, as she called it, from her family who were perturbed about his motivation. He was financially stable to a certain extent, bearing in mind the theatre production industry is as tumultuous as a roller coaster. The adrenaline ride mixed with a fickle audience can leave the boldest of characters with wobbly legs. We surmised the kudos of 'arm candy' drew Aldo to my niece but she has never been and would refuse to be a piece of 'Red Carpet Confection.' Beautiful in her own way sounds so patronising but it is difficult to describe – a stoic beauty. The glitter held no appeal: "sparkle soon fades and sequins fall off," she would pronounce loudly. She did not have a hidden pot of gold or was not in line of a substantial inheritance therefore maybe the age gap was sufficient to fulfil his ego for a while? Aldo went through a period of 'resting' i.e. the offer of roles dried up and the hope of furthering his career or stealing the limelight again was fading. "Just like the leaves in autumn," she used to say to her partner in pursuit of top billing on the stage whether in theatreland or on the big screen. "They turn into a variety of colours and seem darkened to those giving a passing glance however they are an important part of the regrowth and renewal of brighter, fresher, and stronger production in the spring."

"*Don't forget the brittle edges*," her mum whispered under her breath. Joanna heard her mother and ignored her in equal measure. So maybe my niece's words of comfort cushioned the blows for Aldo during his period of reflection i.e. unemployment. The ridiculous reviews of his last role in the production of a play entitled, 'Forget in the Lines,' staged in the Soho Theatre in Dean Street, W1D, were filled with bitterness to attract attention from the public yearning for the next drama. The news cycle flips over with ever increasing speed: to feed the craving for the next new 'thing' whether it be a product or personal. The bad review tends to be forgotten quickly. But critics can inflict deep wounds into the careers of actors gripping onto the tightrope of their dreams especially if their paths have crossed in the distant past. "He has a memory like an elephant," Aldo screeched as he delivered the lines of the crushing review by an old acquaintance. "I thought he would understand better than anyone how I am trying to promote a play by an upcoming playwright. The director specifically asked for me and this is how I am rewarded." The recollection was not quite accurate because Aldo's agent was only able to secure this role whilst other opportunities were on the back burner. The congenial relationship between the critic and Aldo soured when they both auditioned for the same role for a theatre production in Shaftesbury Avenue. Aldo's success in securing the role, attracting rave reviews, and soaring box office sales led to an acrimonious de-coupling. An accusation of cronyism and gossip filled the large net cast out to the local newspapers, but the press did not take the bait. One could say they did not want to miss out on the possibility of free tickets, not that ever happens of course! Therefore, a bitter actor fell and threatened retaliation in a memoir. When a publisher could not be found, the move to be a theatre critic proved to be an ideal act of retaliation. Aldo's career was already in decline before the acidic article, covered by a blanket of perceived professional journalism, was published. It firmly placed Aldo in the waiting room for a lengthy period. Jo stated she thought the name of the play was inappropriate and would attract bad press no matter who was in the starring role. Her attempt to placate her partner did not ease his exasperation in fact it intensified his anger due to the lack of her understanding of the premise of the play. The title represented how we need to improvise in life when we forget where we are and at times need to be prompted to move on to the next line. However, her care and misplaced devotion to him, helped cushion the blows and this served a purpose until he returned to the limelight. She was a distraction. Also, an attraction to agents who could use her to promote his new roles. He did teach her about tricks of the trade, and they attended workshops for her benefit. Aldo found them extraordinarily tedious but endured them to keep her interested and by his side until he could move onto the next stage in his life. Promises were made and broken with regards them moving around the country together when plays went on tour. His longstanding agent did not give up on him and put him forward for a role in Edinburgh. His audition was successful, and a one-way solo rail ticket was purchased. My niece's public façade started to crack when the telephone calls ceased and the anticipated new flat in the outskirts of Edinburgh did not materialise. If her mother or me asked her to forget about Aldo there was an abrupt response, and her stubbornness entrenched her into further distress. "Don't you understand how busy he is?" Her stern voice increased the volume to such an extent our ears could not tolerate an elongated argument.

Jo's father was not interested in her broken heart. "She makes her bed; she lies in it." He mused and muttered.

"Well, there you go. Problem solved!" his ex-wife snapped her reply during their telephone conversation. "Your fatherly love is still absent from your daughter's life, or should I say, your eldest daughter's life. I'm sure your new daughter gets all the attention she wants when you can tear yourself away from making the next deal!"

Tarquin shouted, "I DO NOT HAVE TIME FOR AN ARGUMENT." He paused for effect: leaving enough time for the guilt-ridden blow to land. "What, exactly, do you expect me to do whilst you're swanning around in Italy with your toy boy?"

My sister took a deep breath and said each word with intensity, "Jo will not have a bed to lie on soon. Aldo's selling his flat and wants her out before Christmas. She can stay with Sebastian for a while, but they are going away during the school holidays. And Jo doesn't want to commute from Kenley."

"Why they going away for Christmas? Won't be able to see my grandchildren," he moaned.

"It's not bothered you before!" A distraught and protective mother rebuked her ex-husband. "Hate to state the obvious but you are an Estate Agent, surely you can find Jo a flat?"

"I know I'm good, but even I can't magic a property out of thin air at such short notice. Do you have any idea the price of property in central London?" Tarquin asked.

"No, I don't but you cannot put a price on the number of years you missed from your children's lives and the missed child support payments."

"Oh, for goodness' sake! Change the record," Tarquin groaned. "I've explained the circumstances time and time again. If you don't want to listen that is your problem. Right, I have a viewing in ten minutes, so I'll call Joanna this afternoon. She won't answer and won't reply as per usual, but I'll send her a WhatsApp. It's up to her, if she needs help, she'll have to talk to me. Simple! Why doesn't angel Aunty Mary perform a miracle? She thinks she can save the world."

"She's busy taking care of dad. Funny enough, I thought Jo's father might want to help!" My sister's sarcastic tone was met with an abrupt end to the call.

The death of my dad prompted Jo into action. My sister, Eadgifu – known as Edie, and me set up an amateurish removal firm comprising of a hire van and second-hand packing boxes and suitcases. Jo did not want assistance from her stepfather who travelled to London for my dad's funeral. She did not want assistance from any relatives. She could not cope with enquiring eyes nor awkward questions during the process of moving to her new home in Marylebone. Her father initially paid a nominal rent for the flat until all the legal paperwork for the sale was completed in the spring of 2023. At least there was a benefit from the network of his contacts. Edie suspects the purchase is the first step on the ladder of his proposed property portfolio. I feel sorry for those walking under the ladder. It will be bad luck for the new tenant. For now, it is used as an investment not an interest in his daughter's welfare. Tarquin has no intention in changing the name on the lease to his daughter.

Although there have been many changes during the years since my sister had her son and daughter some things do not change i.e. Edie wants Jo to get a steady, 9 to 5 job like her brother, and Jo thinks her mother's name is stupid. "Did not have much choice as a baby," my sister repeated at each opportunity she got to speak to her daughter which was quite a rarity. "Nan chose the name Eadgifu after an historical figure – Eadgifu of Kent who was the third wife of Edward the Elder, King of Wessex. Nan and Grandad were interested in history."

"Blah, blah, blah," Jo yawned disrespectfully and then said, "Could have changed your name by deed poll when you were eighteen?"

"What? And upset your Nan and Grandad for my own vanity?"

"Doesn't matter!" Jo replied petulantly "We've all got silly names."

"If that's the case," I said, "you could change your name from Jo to Joy?"

My niece rolled her eyes and muttered, "give me strength!"

I laughed and continued whilst trying to avoid my niece's piercing stare. "Is Mary plain enough for you? Dad chose my middle name, Estella. He told me the inspiration was the character in the novel Great Expectations."

Jo's body language and facial expression brightened briefly. She shared a memory, "Aldo once played the part of Mr Jaggers. He got great reviews." Her voice trailed off weakly, and she quickly wiped the tear drops from her cheeks and went to the bathroom.

"Leave her!" Edie mouthed and pushed another box in my direction.

"MUM!" Jo called out. "What have you done with my shampoo?"

"It's in Mary's rucksack!" Edie replied.

"Don't be stupid! There's no space in Aunty's bag. Goodness knows what she has in there?" Jo quipped. "Have to wash my hair; got a meeting this afternoon. Cosimo needs to go through the progress on the scenery and lights."

"Jo, darling, it's your move day, can't they give you at least one day off?" An anxious mother expressed her disquiet openly, but I cringed, and my face crumpled, because Jo despises being called darling by her mother. I assume she is more relaxed when the word is used by her colleagues and/ or her latest boyfriend.

"There's plenty of shops on your doorstep," I said. "Tell me what you need, and I'll go and get some supplies." I thought it an apt moment to give Edie and Jo space, in hope they would have a long overdue conversation. I was too naïve.

***

"*She is thirty-five*," I say to myself in the mirror. "*She is not a baby!*"

Joanna puts on a good front but behind the scenes the turmoil of her parents' divorce disrupts her thought pattern and decision-making process.

Although academically bright, Jo stood in the shadow of her older brother, Sebastian, Charles, whose names were selected by his father without consultation or consideration for his wife. The first name had to be one of his father's middle names which comprised of Sebastian, Jonathan, and Rowland. The name, Charles, was in tribute to Prince Charles. When Sebastian met his wife Sophia and she revealed her middle name is Frances, Tarquin pronounced loudly that it was his choice to include Charles on his son's birth certificate and he must be able to see into the future. I chuckled when Jo said "he thinks he is mystic Meg and that is an insult to her. Only fortune teller he is interested in is the one that will make his fortune!" She was and still is straight to the point. The guests at Sebastian and Sophia's wedding looked perplexed at the excitement of the estranged father about his daughter-in-law's name. Tarquin revelled in laying out how Prince Charles married Lady Diana Frances Spencer in 1981, the year Sebastian was born. He repeated himself slowly in a patronising manner until everyone nodded their heads in hope, he would change the subject or would go back to the bar. My sister was immune to her ex-husband's behaviour to a certain extent but could not stop him going to his son's wedding. As the reception drew to a close, the happy couple left to cheers and applause and shouts of "Congratulations! Have a great honeymoon! Don't forget to send a postcard." The DJ announced the last song of the night, "Last Waltz" by Engelbert Humperdinck. The remainder of the guests danced, and others staggered around the floor. As the lights came back up and the smudged make up was revealed as well as the dishevelled ties, Tarquin shouted to Joanna, "You next, sweetheart! Don't know though? No one will put up with you!"

My sister grabbed Tarquin by the arm with one hand and snatched his jacket from the back of a chair with the other. "Get out!" she whispered severely.

"Oh darlin'! Not finished my champagne." His wimpish reply infuriated my sister even more.

"Get out now or I'm going to call the police or better still will tell your dad about your floundering career."

Tarquin mumbled colourful expletives and stumbled out onto the pavement.

"Save that language for your mates," Edie snarled. "Wait a minute. You ain't got any mates; only those poor people you work with. What do you call them? 'Buddy'? Don't think so.!"

"Shut up. You old witch." Tarquin's scathing retort was met with the door slammed in his face.

***

Joanna left school at the age of sixteen much to the aghast of her mother and grandparents. She did not share the same enthusiasm for establishment education as she called it. "Brainwashing!" she shrieked when asked to re-consider. Dad offered to pay for her to go on holiday for one month with her friend, Minty (short for Araminta). Time to reflect and hopefully change her mind. My nomination as a chaperone was as much as a surprise to Jo as to me. I even got to the point of negotiating unpaid leave with the director, at work, subject to completing the objectives of stage two of the data conversion project. My seventeen years in the insurance company in the City of London, swayed the authorisation to a certain extent. We hoped Minty would do one more favour for the family after intervening to stop the bullying in school on more than one occasion. Minty had a settled, strong family structure. She could tell the bullies, "I'll tell my dad about you." Her father was a loving protective role model unlike Jo's father who just told his daughter "Give as good as you get!" Dad offered to pursue the legal route with the school governors to ensure they were following their '*duty of care*' obligation. We had every confidence that dad: a Barrister Q.C., would win the case and ensure the necessary action was taken, but Edie could not keep Jo away from school during this potentially lengthy process. And word would soon get out that Jo had made a complaint or more commonly known as '*grassing them up.*' Minty's mother knew the family of the leader of the bully gang and broached the subject with diplomacy and direct determination; to convey the message that the behaviour will not be tolerated. Jo stayed at home, indeed spent most of the time in her bedroom, for a couple of weeks. The teachers rearranged the timetable for each pupil, where practical, including sports activities which Jo despised. The mini sabbatical from school was recorded but was not the subject of an in-depth review, nor fine, nor the need for the parents to have a meeting with the headmistress. Not that Tarquin would have attended – his mantra is, "time is money." In his view the rearrangements were a waste of time, especially his time. because everyone knew Joanna would be leaving school soon. Minty's mother met the two close friends at the gate at the end of each school day and drove them directly to the safety of her home. Jo tried to rebel against the perceived restrictive terms and conditions of the protective care but when the alternative was set out in front of her, the reality hit home. Minty had a talent for music. Jo loved singing songs whilst Minty played beautiful melodies on the piano in the spare bedroom. The regular, home cooked meals helped reduce Jo's interest in the latest fashionable diet craze, which she intermittently tested, during the impressionable teenage years. She came to realise the simple equation of 'eat less – move more,' was the answer. Thankfully, she does not have any health conditions which unbalance that equation. Edie juggled work commitments with the care of her children. Tarquin deserted his family to start a new life with his youthful mistress. She was a potential buyer. Not the stereotypical secretary or ex-girlfriend.

In 2004, when Jo celebrated her long awaited sixteenth birthday, Sebastian was studying at The University of Surrey. He is a stable character who did not carry the weight of his parent's divorce and arguments on his shoulders. He was the favourite grandchild and was extremely happy to stay with his great granddad and grandma in their cosy, country, cottage located in Tandridge in East Surrey. The descriptive of 'cottage' did not reflect the expansive size of the property and garden. As Tarquin would say, "trigger words, trigger dreams, and trigger commission." Unfortunately, these tacky phrases tend to stick in your mind like the annoying tune you cannot get out of your head.

Gilbert, Albert, Frederick, Danrich, was my loving paternal grandfather. A successful Barrister Q.C. concluding his prestigious career as Head of Chambers. On the rare occasion Jo did stay, grandma would enthusiastically share the background of the family tree:

"Great grandpa was named after Sir George Gilbert Scott. The famous architect who designed The Albert Memorial. Do you remember when we went to the Festival of Remembrance at The Royal Albert Hall with grandpa and Sebastian?" Jo nodded dutifully.

"I must go and find the photographs; it was a lovely sunny day." Grandma said, hoping it would awaken an interest in her great-granddaughter. Jo remembered the magnificent displays of military precision and how the music touched the ceiling – orchestrated by the incredible acoustics, however the photographs had faded into a distant memory.

"Sebastian was intrigued by the details of the design of The Albert Memorial, including the carved figures of Pugin and Giotto. Oh my, the names of all the great curators have slipped my mind. The book is in our study. Sebastian is such a good student and learned about all the different aspects of the masterpiece." Jo stifled a yawn and looked towards her feet tucked into the navy blue, hand knitted, pom-pom slippers. Grandma was gifted with skills to knit and sew and cook: her cakes were legendary. Unfortunately, none of us inherited all those skills. But in fairness, Edie is a good all-round cook, and dad made a superb burnt bacon sandwich hidden in tomato sauce. Although, it was no match for my pickled onion sandwiches, especially on Boxing Day.

Jo loved learning to play the piano at her great-grandparent's home. There was a grand piano in the extremely spacious lounge and when the keys were continuously hit in the wrong order, Sebastian would hide in the study and thrived on reading the eclectic selection of books in the floor to ceiling bookshelves. Grandpa and Grandma patiently tolerated the strange musical arrangements and enjoyed Jo's impersonations of famous actors and admired her incredible ear for different accents. Her performances raised howls of laughter during the traditional game of Charades at Christmas. The applause from the small audience encouraged her to be even more theatrical. She had a talent for acting and it was visible from an early age – as a toddler she turned a smile into a frown within a blink of an eye. Once the awkward, self-conscious teenage years took over, she gradually withdrew from family games, preferring to listen to songs on her Walkman, or more often than not, going to her bedroom to watch films on the television.

Grandpa hoped Sebastian would follow in his keen interest in cricket. Sebastian absorbed the history of the Outwood Cricket Club, in Tandridge, formed in 1887 and still active. However, he developed into a fan of football much to grandpa's disappointment.

Jo's apprenticeship in the Shaftesbury Theatre in London's West End, started with show-related work: an assistant to Wardrobe and Make-Up, then moving onto stage design. She was eager to learn and willing to help with a variety of tasks She thought a conscientious attitude and multi-tasking ability when under pressure, against the clock, would help her achieve the dream of being a director of a play. Work hard and long hours, surely, it would reap rewards. Nothing quite prepared her for how tough the industry is, and the critique can be quite brutal at times. Networking is a vital component, but the socialising required spending a great deal of time with people who you would rather not know and spending a great deal of money on drinks. The new contacts were not always happy to go to the pub and insisted on going to trendy cocktail bars. Dad would bankroll a select few of the evenings and I would reluctantly grant a loan to Jo but rarely saw a return. I refused to apply for a joint credit card or open a joint bank account which resulted in the silent treatment for a few weeks.

Joanna enrolled in a Foundation Course to train as an actor, in Dean Street, Soho. The flexibility in the timetable enabled her to take on extra tasks in preparing the stage scenery. She learnt the lines for each character, in the faint hope that she may be called upon to be an understudy. One frustrated actor kept forgetting his lines and his health deteriorated due to the stress. Jo pounced on the opportunity and was stunned when the director agreed to give her an audition and offered her the role for one week until they could find a full-time replacement. One established actor-ideal for the part was contracted to be in another production for a further three weeks. The director hoped a couple of members of the cast could learn all the lines within one week. Jo secretly hoped they would not be able to learn the lines and the contract for the experienced actor would be extended. Sadly, her aspirations did not come true, and she returned to working backstage after a fairly good performance in a traditional male role which included dancing. The director was impressed and jokingly said she was a 'Triple Threat' i.e. she could act, dance and sing. He said in a condescending tone, "don't forget to thank me in your Oscar acceptance speech."

The production team were introduced to the new actor, Aldo Fabrizzi. Jo's liaison with Aldo started earlier than we thought. She was hypnotised by his charm and yearned for his stardom. He was fascinated by the trainee and the chase began to snare this young lady. The fact he was married was a minor inconvenience.

***

Jo works as a freelancer and is free in spirit but trapped by the fear of ending up as emotionally scarred as her mother. In a moment of foolish frustration, I told my niece, "an alcoholic hides in a bottle and a workaholic hides at work."

The scathing response was not a surprise. "Where do you hide? Oh, that's right. In your flat. A future husband is not going to knock on your door and say, 'do you come here often?'"

Edie thinks I am a bad influence on my niece – she takes after my contrary side, and is rebellious, and has a stubborn nature. I refute the claims. Dad said I spoilt her when she was a child. I acquiesced to his assessment. I felt sorry for her and maybe she was a substitute child. I never had the same connection with Sebastian however there was a mutual respect. He displayed more manners and had a milder temperament in comparison to his baby sister.

Jo has not been in a truly committed relationship. Well, that is what she says but not what she feels. Bottom line is, she does not trust anyone, stemming from the twisted roots of her father's behaviour and compounded by the antics of Aldo. Not really a shock that she got entangled with a man who has the same characteristic traits as Tarquin. Jo is a complex character but at her core is a considerate and loving nature: well-hidden gems. It will take dedicated hard graft to mine the rocks and clean them. But they are worth all the sweat and tears, as long as there is not a landslide before the gems are found. Not many men have the strength and determination to achieve the task. More fool them – they are the losers. If they want a quick fix, then the clumps of earth soon crumble.

As Jo continues the quest to be a director the added pressure of posting regular updates on her 'socials' as she calls them is relentless. It is draining and deprives her of precious time with her family which is dreadfully sad. Our lives are blighted by '*anti-social*' media. I have been called a frump, a grump, and a lump for holding such views. We are paying a high price for convenience, whether it be in retail or connecting with friends or immediate recognition of attention seeking photos. A life can be changed by pressing the like button: an online round of applause with potential devastating consequences. Can't we see the irony and imagery of the Roman Emperor in the Colosseum making the final decision by showing a thumbs up or down. No matter how exhausted the gladiators are, the blood thirsty crowd are never satisfied.

The curtain is slowly being drawn back, revealing the fallout from virtual social networking and it is frightening.

'FOMO' – Fear of Missing Out is another motivational factor in my niece's life. The extent of peer pressure led to unwise decisions and attracted unwanted attention and compromising positions. Even Jo fell for the tricks and lies.

We thought she was more savvy but emotions are strong. To change the status online to 'in a relationship' albeit for one week is exhilarating. The bubble bursts quickly and when blocked by 'Mr Cool' the onset of the cruel remarks is relentless.

"Why can't you stop it happening?" Jo cried to her mum and me when the trolls took images from her social media accounts and photo shopped them to make her look hideous and it made her a laughing stock.

"Stop it?" I exclaimed. "I can't even start it."

Edie and me vowed to learn more about apps and online activity but we could not keep up. Sebastian stepped in to block accounts and delete images, and negotiate with the individuals in question, to delete their copies or otherwise they could find themselves amidst legal action. Jo resented her brother "taking over" as she called it, but it was far better than her father blurting it out to his work colleagues or her stepmother who would weaponize the weakness in the suit of armour Jo wore during the rare occasions they had the misfortune to be in the same room. There is no guarantee the images will not reappear. Easy to rebuke her and say, "how could you be so silly?" when echoes from the past remind me of the coercive characters and their catchphrases. "Oh, you're a good girl." "Why are you so boring?"

"Go on – it's only a laugh." The images of those times may not be online but are etched in my mind. The humiliation and lack of self-respect, and the pain rise to the surface when stress squeezes into the middle.

The attempts to make Aldo jealous when he was wandering with a new acquaintance did not quite work. Like me, he was not *au fait* with social media therefore he did not see all the photos posted by Jo and when his colleagues showed him a select few images, it was like water of a duck's back. He was the star of the show and Jo was the understudy in both work and in their on and off relationship.

**

CHAPTER 2

Torn pieces of plastic wrapping from bunches of flowers, purchased from the local garage, lay strewn over the paths in the cemetery. New plant pots, secured by larger stones, stayed close to the headstones. An additional gift placed on the modest plot of land to mark another significant milestone.

There are moments when I think it is quite morbid to spend Father's Day in a graveyard instead of spending time with relatives who are alive. However, there are other moments when I think this view is far too judgemental and harsh. Grief is a unique experience. You have to learn to live with it. Some try to forget it, but the stress of the loss tends to rise to the surface and can unleash a storm if the anchor in our lives has been removed from the seabed.

I wanted to miss the usual increased number of visitors on Father's Day, and Jo would not have come even if I bought her two plates full of her favourite waffles. She has lost faith in religion. My measly attempts at explaining there is a chasm between man-made religion and Faith is met with a rebuttal. The content of the replies varies but all are delivered with the same force. The most commonly used phrases are –

"Yeah, if you say so. Move on – next subject."

"When did you become a preacher?"

"Suppose you're after money for the church roof?"

There are other colourful replies but will not repeat them. Even though she dislikes her father immensely and he was not a part of her upbringing, she has inherited his potty mouth. To be fair, she does try to rein in the various shades of blue. Mum and Dad did not tolerate even a slight detour from respectful language. Mum was the leader in this disciplinary measure, and Jo did not forget the consequence when she stepped across the line. Dad had softer edges and was lenient with my rebellious outbursts, too lenient according to mum, but kept to the joint course of action in respect of Jo: funds for the networking social events were stopped for one month. Jo knew not to push her nan so turned in my direction. During moments of weakness, I gave in. She knows which buttons to push. But on the whole, I kept in unison with my parents to show a strong boundary. When mum's health first started to deteriorate, we did not want her upset by Jo's occasional outburst. Mum and dad had no worries about Sebastian which infuriated Jo. Her older brother was the favourite with all our relatives, except for me. Maybe I am looking in the mirror when I see my niece?

The additional engraving on the plain white headstone which was replaced on the settled earth was simple and sentimental. The surface was relatively clean despite the heavy rain. A small picket fence proved to be an effective and aesthetically pleasing way to retain the flower display mum requested – she loved gardening. Two small conifer trees stood proudly each side of the headstone. Columns guarding the entrance to the place of rest.

Sebastian said, "the horticultural name for the conifer is Juniperus communis '*Compressa.*'"

Jo replied, "really? How interesting. We're not in the Chelsea Flower Show."

"You can't help yourself, can you?" Edie, exhausted with the critique, stared at her daughter, and said, "please Jo.

Please, just stop with the cutting remarks for a few moments. Nan loved her garden, and she especially liked these shrubs."

Before Edie had time to take a breath, Jo retorted, "they're small trees not shrubs. You should've paid more attention to your mother."

I grimaced and said, "Oh. I am so tempted. But I'll keep it short and sweet. You can either be respectful or be remote. You choose."

Jo remained silent. Her expression said all that she was thinking. Edie and Sebastian were quite taken aback but relieved that Jo had stopped talking. The awkward atmosphere hung over us like a storm cloud, but I could not tolerate one of Jo's notorious outbursts whilst we were standing at mum and dad's graveside. They made it clear we were not to spend thousands on a headstone which will only fade and crumble. They were pragmatic and prophetic as mum repeatedly told us. "You will eventually move away from the area. In the not-too-distant future, there will be no visitors to maintain the grave, and weeds will overtake the mini-memorial cottage garden."

Dad set in place watertight legal documents and trust funds, to ensure Tarquin did not benefit by one penny from the inheritance.

Our parting messages are –

Rosalind Danrich.
1935 – 2021
Loving wife and mum and grandma.
Blessed with an abundance of gifts – generously shared with us.
Rest peacefully.

Thomas Danrich
1932 – 2022
Loving and loyal husband, dad and granddad.
Eternally grateful for each minute we shared.
You had a good innings!
Rest peacefully.

Two pages of additional tributes were engraved on a free-standing granite memorial book.

"You'll need a mausoleum at this rate." Jo quipped when the idea was first suggested. A fellow trainee in the theatre used her calligraphy skills and the display is marvellous. Edie has reservations and says, out of ear shot of Jo, "looks like a GP's writing. Can't really see the words." Her second, younger, husband disagrees profusely. He thinks the artistry compliments their range of talents and incorporates a tribute to heritage and highlights their genuine interest in history.

Jo inevitably found out about the feedback from her mother and snapped, "what do you want? A billboard with neon lights?" To this day I do not know the source of the leak. Maybe Susie Beatty, our family hairdresser, let it slip during a quick trim. She is not a relative but has been styling our hair for decades in her saloon on the High Street. Susie is a lifelong career hairdresser. She worked in South Molton Street, W1, in earlier years however returned to East Wickham to be near family as she sets the route on the path to retirement. Susie has excellent skills however has dedicated her time to the profession and not her personal life: never married, and no children, but she was engaged once. Her Fiancé abandoned her, to work in Paris. He desired more the perceived prestigious model agency work and to be involved in top brand fashion shows. Susie Beatty did not match his expectation of a *fast pace*. She referred to his idol as a *false face*.

Jo does not have big fancy big hair styles and found it hilarious when I showed her the photos of me with the 'Dynasty' bouffant. Jo stifled her laugh for a few minutes to ask, "what where you watching? No TV show would have hair like that. It would have been banned." She continued to cackle loudly whilst I stuffed the glossy colour photographs back into the cover.

I suspect Tarquin surreptitiously manoeuvred Edie's comments about the calligraphy, onto the platform of social media. The new members of staff in the Estate Agents, eager to impress and susceptible to coercive behaviour could have found a way to upset the apple cart. Tarquin relished in sowing seeds of division between Edie and their children. Any evidence that could be gathered to prove she is an unfit mother helps get him off the hook.

Sebastian halted Jo's progress in her retaliation about the clarity of calligraphy which is only too obvious when the viewer gives the same amount of time concentrating as the artist gives when creating the artwork. He does not usually step in or stand up to his younger sister but could see the distress inscribed on their mother's face.

Edie feels guilty for moving to Italy. She thinks she should have stayed to help take care of mum and dad. After what Edie had been through, we all supported her move and none of us thought she should remain in Kent. Although, during rare moments of doubt, Jo wanted her mum to stay close. Maybe expressing a need for support or a need for a sparring partner when she knocked me out, verbally. Tarquin did not care where his ex-wife was, but the envy showed if you dissected his words. His second, glamourous and youthful, wife proved useful to get attention on his socials and awaken the green-eyed monster in his work colleagues. Annoyed and confused why Edie does not post photos of her modest home, he complains that his family want to stay in contact and the images are a fantastic way to connect. There are gaping holes in this propaganda because his family do not keep in contact nor connect with him. Edie and Domenico have no need to post photoshopped images – the beauty of nature is on their doorstep. The idyllic setting is shared in person with loved ones. Edie asks me, intermittently, to check on Jo's social media accounts which is futile and a ludicrous request because I cannot comprehend all the different cookies, usernames, and passwords. And who on earth thought of the security check which pops up to verify you are human i.e. tick all the boxes with a traffic light or motorbike? I end up playing noughts and crosses and after about the third attempt finally get through to the next page which asks for the password again. I miss using a biro pen and paper. The marks from the blue ink pens, which were *de rigueur* when I started secondary school, stained my fingers and school blouse which created more wash day duties for mum – she was not amused. So, I do not want to revert to them.

Jo warned her brother off from 'spying' on behalf of their mum which is ironic and ungrateful, bearing in mind how much he helped with damage limitation after her risqué posts. Sebastian was not fazed by the reprimand. He concentrates on being a good role model for his two children and supporting his wife who he loves unconditionally.

Edie and me grew up in a comfortable home. Our four-bedroom detached house in Eston Park Avenue, near Elmar Park Village, in East Wickham in Kent was complimented by a long garden. Dad built a trellis to divide the garden. The pink climbing roses smelt and looked divine however dad's motivation for the outdoor DIY project was not taken from the iconic television programme, Gardeners' World presented by Percy Thrower, but more by the opportunity to build a 'man cave' out of sight of the kitchen window. The proposed shed turned out to be a type of Chalet which we all loved. A slight cause of frustration for dad because this was meant to be 'his space.' Determined not to be defeated, dad paid for a professional gardener to redesign the half of the garden closest to the house. As a treat dad said we could choose one item of garden furniture each. Edie settled on a slide, and I selected a swinging two-seater in a floral cotton covering with matching sunshade. Mum chose a new set of garden furniture and a large yellow umbrella, with white frilly edging, which was an extremely popular attraction for the wasps so had to be changed for a pastel blue one. Special privilege was given to mum because she was not only a magnificent housekeeper but managed all the social events for our family so had the superior knowledge with regards the most suitable design and size to fit on the new patio which was a last-minute addition to the garden makeover. Dad insisted the Victorian style conservatory had to stay, although showing wear and tear, because his parents adored the style and sentimental memories of when it was used as a playroom for Edie and me. Quite a high-risk strategy, putting us in a space with such large windows. The soft indoor cricket ball was purchased after an accidental breakage when we were playing with a small but heavier football. The idea of an indoor penalty shootout seemed great fun, as the heavy rain tapped on the roof panels and dripped through the emerging cracks in the ornamental cresting. Edie criticised my goalkeeping skills and said I should have caught the ball. I retaliated by pointing out that she kicked the ball way over the make-shift net – two cardigans on the floor and a cushion balancing on the back of the settee. Grandma introduced us to painting and embroidery to keep us distracted from any more indoor sporting competitions – she blamed grandpa for telling us about cricket. I am not sure where the interest from football came from – most likely peer pressure from school or from Edie's school friends. I was not as social as Edie and never had a group of friends. Although Edie was only three years older, we seemed to be a generation apart.

I could not pronounce my older sister's name – Eadgifu, so we called her Edie which she preferred: made it much easier during morning registration in school. Due to historical significance of Eadgifu, grandma called her Queen of the Castle which tormented me especially when Edie teased me by saying I would be an excellent servant.

The original choice of a middle name was Rose, to describe a beautiful baby but mum wanted to change it to Rosa because it of the charming style and musicality. Also, in recognition of Salvator Rosa (1615 – 1673). Rosa was one of the least conventional artists of 17th-century Italy. Rosa worked in Florence and its neighbourhood from 1640 – 1649, before returning to Rome, where he eventually died, A prophetic choice of name. Her other name was Elizabeth. A tribute to the tradition in mum's family i.e. named in honour of our late and much-loved Queen Elizabeth II who was born in 1926. I think many girls in my mum's generation had Elizabeth somewhere on their birth certificate. As far as I can remember our family had an overtly keen interest in names and their historical significance which has stuck in our psyche. That level of interest has not even reached the sides of Jo's mind however she tolerates a minute or two of reminiscing. It is stated firmly that she sat through tedious hours of testimony by her nan and great grandma so will not put up with listening to repetitive rattling on. On rare occasions, we repeat her statement when she spends hours talking about her latest boyfriend. This was most prolific when accounts of Aldo's achievements were broadcast on continuous cycles. When in a good mood Jo relinquishes and says, "touché."

At the age of three Edie adjusted to my intrusion into her home with caution and tantrums. I think she would have preferred a baby brother and sometimes sense my mum felt the same. Dad was extremely pleased his wonderful wife and new baby were safe and well. He did not cherish the thought of managing a home and his career although grandma would have taken charge He most certainly did not want to move further outside of London and grandma would not have moved to East Wickham. He need not have worried. I took a lot longer to arrive than Edie, and mum was considered to be a fairly mature mother at the age of twenty-eight, in that time frame. Mum's recovery was enhanced after a week in hospital – to enable her to heal from the medical intervention. A type of convalescent care not usually offered in the present day. Dad brought Edie to visit mum in hospital. She cried when she saw her mother, and inappropriately laughed when she left, with her new large panda bear she named Graham. Dad suggested Gemima, but Edie thought that was a silly name so that was one name excluded from the options for my birth certificate. Edie peeked over the edge of the cot as I slept; looked at my bright red chubby cheeks, pulled at my pink hat which was hand knitted by Grandma and then turned her attention back to Graham.

The names selected for me were Mary Estella Bernadette. My first name selected as a tribute to grandma and mum i.e. their middle names. But a name used to tease me throughout childhood. I still hear echoes of "Mary, Mary, quite contrary how does your garden grow?" Although an apt description when childhood tantrums took over and reappeared during the teenage transition to an adult. The foot stomping may have changed from an actual activity to a metaphoric gesture but the attention seeking rears its ugly head occasionally.

Estella is based on a character in Great Expectations by Charles Dickens: a seemingly cold and distant girl but her icy exterior blocks the love she retains for Pip. Dad chose the name – an insight into his interest in English Literature. He enjoyed the film adaption starring John Mills. Dad used to say the final scene of the old movie is an ideal setting and depicts the essence of the story.I cannot recall the reason for the choice of Bernadette. Jo will probably remember and pronounce loudly, "how can I forget? It was drummed into me."

My sister sailed through Grammar school. I wore water wings throughout each day which needed to be reinflated now and then when I fell below the water line. I got through school years and 'O' Level exams by the skin of my teeth. There was no point in staying and little chance of passing 'A' Levels. My French teacher, Madame Cabasse earnestly tried to change my mind. I was tempted but could not justify continuing the torment of going to school based on one award winning essay, and grade A in the spoken French exam. Mum and grandma were horrified at my decision. Dad and grandpa were disappointed but realistic. They saw and accepted that the pressure was getting to me. I told my family. "It's like putting a square peg into a round hole." Edie proclaimed her agreement rather too quickly for my liking but gave some weight to the argument.

I left school at sixteen. Edie blames me for being a bad influence on Jo. "You started it" she says in moments of frustration. "You know she idolises you!" "Don't be silly" I reply, "she insults me." Edie needs to land the blame at someone's feet for the fact that Jo did not want to go to university like her brother.

Edie was more studious achieving 'A' levels in History, Art, and Drama but the results were not all straight A* grades which demotivated her and eventually led to the decision to leave full time education at eighteen. Her 'O' Level results were proportionally better, in her mind. At the age of sixteen boys were a distraction but did not take away the ability to pass exams. Her intelligence surpassed visits to the disco and cinema. She had a few boyfriends – nothing too serious. Taller and thinner than me, her beauty attracted a lot of attention. She was flirty but not foolish to the extent of an unplanned pregnancy which blighted the life of a couple of girls in school. Strangely the fathers; uncomfortable to refer to a fifteen-year-old boy as a father, did not have to make life changing decisions. They rejected responsibility and relationship.

One month before my sixteenth birthday the career advisor went through the box standard options for a female with an expectation of reasonable 'O' Level results i.e. typist, supermarket cashier and administration clerk without defining a specific business or company. I took the handful of papers and put them in my pending file in my bedroom – bottom drawer of dressing table which Grandma gave me. I regarded the style of the furniture to be old fashioned and boring but in retrospect the vintage design was delightful. I regret donating the dressing table to a charity shop. I thought the mdf flat pack chest of drawers would make a far more effective storage space and fit just nicely in the corner of my one-bedroom flat. But Grandma's dressing table stored memories and showcased the tradition of our family. I was too quick to give it away albeit for a worthy cause. Just one regret of many. I kept the elegant, hinged mirror which used to sit comfortably on grandma's dressing table. The three reflected images framed in brass made a sublime sun catcher.

***

CHAPTER 3

One month after my sixteenth birthday mum and dad passed me the daily newspapers and I promised to send at least one application per week to prospective employers. There were various vacancies advertised in the civil service, so I sent letters to the Home Office and Ministry of Defence. The invitation to an interview by the Metropolitan Police seemed quite exciting upon receipt of the correspondence but when facing the panel of four officials my mouth dried and I did not dare pick up the glass of water balancing on the desk in case I dropped it. Enquiries were made as to my plans in respect of further education, and I reassured them my aim was to go to evening school. My interview attire: a grey two-piece skirt suit with fine white pin stripes, bought by mum in John Lewis, was dry-cleaned before my interview with Britus Life Assurance company located near Trafalgar Square. Miss Drake, the manager of Drying Days & Sewing Streams, refreshed the outfit and tidied up a few loose threads on the hem of the skirt.

It was an extraordinarily brief interview with the manager of HR. A pleasant, petite, and prim character named Miss Hamilton shook my hand softly and gestured to me to sit on the small office chair opposite her pristine desk. She showed great interest in architecture of my school building rather than the subjects of my exams – she skipped over the details on my application with a pleasant smile. She was fascinated by dad's career and almost asked me why I did not follow his footsteps into law, but you could see the balance of acceptable questions being weighed up in her eyes. The topic of conversation turned to my hobbies and why

I wanted to work in central London. I explained my attendance at the dancing school in Sydenham came to a halt when studying for exams escalated and my Saturday shifts at the Cancer Research Charity shop clashed with the weekend lessons. I failed to mention that the lack of teenage boy partners in the lessons sort of put a dampener on the excitement of dancing in a professional studio. It was more the humiliation of being paired with ten and twelve-year-old boys who were not only more stylish than me but had already achieved silver medal awards. Mum thought working in a charity shop would be good training for interacting with different characters and a chance to improve my multi-tasking skills. I tried to persuade dad that I could do homework and watch television at the same time and practise dance steps whilst cleaning the kitchen – one household duty to obtain extra 'pocket money.' Dad referred the appeal to mum, but she did not change her judgement. Mum said when I could go to bigger and brighter dance studios in central London but only after I had signed up to evening classes in business studies.

Miss Hamilton appeared to be impressed with my answers. She took me on an unexpected tour of the large building which resembled a museum rather than the dreaded drab office. The high heels of my new grey shoes clattered on the large stone staircase and echoed towards the large leaded glass dome skylight ceiling. I apologised to all the staff who passed by and tried to balance on tip toes but that did not prove to be a successful strategy because I stumbled and almost tumbled over. I gripped the cold iron circular handrail and coughed in an attempt to provide a distraction from my athletic descent

"You alright darlin'? Steady as you go. Has Sue been sharing her special brew again?"

Miss Hamilton stared at the suave tall gentleman with a distinctive moustache and a bouffant hair style. His light brown hair appeared to have blonde highlights in the quiff. His brown eyes locked into my direction and the beaming white teeth elongated the smile. Slightly spoiled by the chewing gum but assumed it was used to try to hide the smell of cigarettes, but it was not a successful tactic.

"Good morning, Mick," Miss Hamilton replied. "Mary is absolutely fine. We are having a tour of the building and all being well she may be our new colleague soon."

"Looking forward to it," Mick replied, and his smile broadened. I had a niggly feeling it was tinged with a mixture of leering but dismissed my thoughts and put it down to my nerves.

Miss Hamilton tapped my arm to disrupt the moment and said, "I'll show you the restaurant and we can get a cup of tea and biscuits." She saw Mick's face light up and intervened on his thoughts, "the invitation is not for you. Oh yes, forgot to mention. Eric needs the month end report on his desk by Wednesday. He will not tolerate any more delays to his schedule." Mick appeared despondent and reluctantly nodded to acknowledge the critical deadline.

"I apologise," Miss Hamilton said. "There was no intention in you getting caught in the middle of that type of conversation. Whilst we are on this floor, I will check if Eric is in his office and can introduce you to him. If your application is successful, he will be your director." I gulped and smiled politely.

The formal offer of a job from? Insurance Company was on the door mat within one week which was a fast turnaround because I was still awaiting replies from the Civil Service.

"Well done," dad applauded as he celebrated my achievement.

"They have to take on a certain quota of school dropouts," Edie teased.

Mum tutted and reprimanded my older sister which was unusual." Now, now, Edie. Envy is not attractive. Mary must have impressed the HR manager and the director to get a reply so quickly. We will have another bread winner in the house. Why don't you join us?"

I sniggered, and Edie stomped off in a huff.

The first day in the office was surreal. Three new starters and me sat in a large meeting room with a shiny dark oak wood table. I tried to make polite small talk, but the other teenagers seemed to be frozen with fear. I poured out four glasses of water from the large bottle in the centre of the table. There were no takers. I sipped from my glass and tried not to slurp amidst the awkward silence which was deafening.

"Good morning," Miss Hamilton called out as she entered the room. "I apologise for keeping you waiting. My previous meeting over ran. Last minute changes to the schedule. Anyway, are you all well?"

We nodded in unison and did not utter a word.

"That's good. We have temporary work in various departments until the final arrangements have been for your new roles. Richard, Lucy and Jackie, please follow me. Premium Collection need help sending out follow up letters and making the tea."

Jackie blushed, and her handbag slipped onto the floor.

"No need to worry," Miss Hamilton said reassuringly. "Richard will make the tea. I have it on good authority from his mum that he is a whizz in the kitchen." The tension on their faces eased. "Mary, I will be back soon. If you need the facilities, they are just over to the right."

"Thank you," I replied. Although grateful for the space to breathe and stretch my legs, it took a while for the penny to drop – the reference to facilities meant lavatory.

Miss Hamilton took me to the Accounts Department on the top floor. The gated lifts were intriguing and scary, but at least I did not have to navigate the stone staircase.

"Good morning, Chris," said Miss Hamilton as she walked into the office of the Account Manager, Mr Reed. "May I introduce you to your new temporary member of staff, Mary."

"Good morning, Mary, how are you?" Mr Reed said quite sternly.

"Good thank you," I replied. "How are you?" I pressed my lips together tightly and thought, 'was I being too informal and too forward?'

Mr Reed smiled and said, "welcome to Accounts. I hope you passed your maths exam?"

Miss Hamilton interjected to prevent an awkward conversation. "We have not received Mary's results yet, but we are confident that she will pass all nine 'O' Levels. I'm afraid we can only loan you an extra member of staff for one month. The team in Policy Payments are eagerly awaiting their new recruit."

"Yes, of course," Mr Reed said in an appreciative manner. "Eric will not let me forget this favour."

Miss Hamilton laughed lightly and with experience said, "he most certainly will not let you off the hook lightly."

The insight into Eric's characteristics troubled me. I pondered, 'maybe I should have stayed in school?'

"Okay. I need to go," Miss Hamilton said as she looked at the Rolex watch on her left wrist. "Any problems Mary, please telephone my secretary. We are here to support you. In the meantime, I will leave you in the capable hands of Chris. Have a good day."

"Thank you for all your help." My reply did not reach the ears of Miss Hamilton as she walked at pace towards the lift.

I naively thought Mr Reed would give me more details about the history of the company and how long he had worked in the Accounts Department.

"Please take a seat," Mr Reed said as took off the jacket of his brown tweed three-piece suit. "I'm just going to ask Debbie to join us."

The office had grey metal filing cabinets leaning against two of the walls. A large window took up most of the space of the outer wall and a frosted glass panel acted as a divider between the desks and the corridor. I stood up when Debbie came into the office.

"Hello. Nice to meet you," Debbie said. "Really good to get some help. Has Chris explained what you will be doing?"

Mr Reed replied on my behalf, "no. I thought it best to leave all that to you Debbie. You are far better at these things. So, Mary. I will leave you in Debbie's capable hands."

I did not immediately recognise the signs of Debbie's exaggerated laugh and reddened face. The body language was easy to recognise in the television dramas, but in real life it was more difficult to detect especially on my first day.

"Chris, would you like a coffee?" Debbie asked Mr Reed.

"I thought you'd never ask?" Mr Reed smiled mischievously, and I felt increasingly awkward at the exchange of glances. "Debbie, please show Mary where the coffee machine is. A vital part of the training."

I followed Debbie to the corridor with the extremely shiny parquet floor. "I mustn't slip when carrying the drinks." I thought and hoped a positive vision would help me keep my balance.

"We can't just get one drink without asking the others," Debbie said. "I'll go and get the orders and the tray. Press the button for your drink, don't have to wait. Mick usually takes five minutes to make up his mind or should I say, wind me up."

"Did I hear my name taken in vain?" A rasping voice called out as he entered the kitchen area. Well, not really a kitchen. The area consisted of a drinks machine, a vending machine, and a small sink with only one tap giving out cold water.

"Oh, not you," Debbie chuckled. "Our Mick."

"Hello darlin.' We meet again. It's my lucky day."

"You two know each other?" Debbie said with a quizzical look on her face.

"No. Yes. Sorry, not really." My bumbled response raised a laugh amongst our ad-hoc tea party. "Sorry. Miss Hamilton introduced us on the stairs."

"Sue does pick some strange places to have meetings," Debbie laughed.

"Not really a meeting, was it darlin'? You were on your way to see Eric. Did he bite your head off?" The tall man with the bouffant hair style, which was brushed even higher, fixed his attention on me. The white collar of his navy shirt made a suitable ledge for his hair to settle on. "I'm only joking. Eric is a cuddly bear under that harsh exterior."

"He'll be a grizzly bear, if you don't get that report finished." Debbie said with angst across her face.

"No worries. Now we have an extra pair of hands we'll all the outstanding work done." Mick said with an air of confidence bordering on arrogance.

"Keep your hands off Mary," Debbie coughed out of sheer embarrassment. "Sorry. I mean Mary is helping Chris first. I think for about a month."

"I am a patient man," Mick said with a broad smile. "Looking forward to showing her the ropes."

"Give her a break, "Debbie earnestly requested. "It's only her first day."

"Welcome to the world of insurance. Come along on Friday evening? I'll buy you a drink to celebrate."

"Friday? "I asked tentatively.

"It's alright darlin' there'll be a group of us, not just you and me, sadly. Debbie is a regular. You'll show her won't you Debs?"

"Yes," Debbie replied impatiently." But first, can you show Mary how to use the coffee machine? And warn her about the hot chocolate! I must go and get the tray."

The chime from the clock tower of St Martin-in-the-Fields marked the end of the working day. At 5 p.m. the staff in the Accounts Department left the office. I remained seated at my small desk in the corner by the window. There were five more pages to complete before finalising the task allocated to me after lunch. Debbie said I could take a couple of days, but I felt the need to stay because most of the morning had been taken up with settling into the new environment. The antiquated adding machine with the handle on the right side, fascinated me. The paper receipt showed all the entries so I could reconcile the numbers at the end of each page. For some reason I found this rewarding. At 5.45 p.m. I gently knocked on the manager's office door and said, "Excuse me Mr Reed. I have finished the work Debbie gave me. Is it okay if I leave the office now?"

"Yes, of course, well done," he replied. "Debbie is a hard task master. Hope she hasn't frightened you off and you'll come back tomorrow?"

"Thank you, Mr Reed. I look forward to returning to the office."

"That is good to hear. You better be careful otherwise I will want to keep you to myself. But best not, Eric will be fuming."

I blushed and said, "Good night, Mr Reed."

"Please. Call me Chris. Good night, Mary."

Debbie looked quite a different person with the accentuated make up. The chitter chatter of the office workers filtered through the air as we walked towards the Embankment. "Did you get through to your mum?" Debbie asked. I felt slightly agitated and insulted by the question because in my mind I was no longer a school pupil. I was an adult who had every right to go out with her colleagues to celebrate her first week at work. "There was no reply. Dad is working late as usual, and my sister is out with her friends. I left a message with the hairdresser."

"Hairdresser?" Debbie's confused expression prompted my explanation.

"Oh, sorry. Susie, the hairdresser, is a friend. I think mum has an appointment this evening. If not, Susie will find a way to get a message to mum."

"As long as someone knows where you are," Debbie replied.

It seemed an odd statement. Upon reflection a sixteen-year-old girl going into a pub, in the centre of London, which had mostly older male customers was not wise. The thick layer of cigarette smoke hung above the bar which was hidden by a crowd baying for attention from the barmaid. I overheard jibes of "get them in, it's your round." And "make mine a double, it'll last a few weeks until you buy another drink." The banter continued amongst the male office workers wearing crumpled suits from a long week travelling in trains crammed with passengers. The top button undone and loosened tie signalled their break for freedom from the set schedule of the working week.

"There you are. Where've you been?" The enquiry came from an elderly gentleman wearing an expensive, black, double-breasted two-piece suit made from a mixture of wool and silk-blend twill. His highly polished shoes stood out amongst the other scuffed shoes of the tired businessmen.

"We've been busy, haven't we?" Debbie replied and looked at me. "Lots of files to reconcile before the deadline next week." I nodded to reaffirm the excuse for our late arrival although I was not aware of a set start time of Friday night drinks.

"Debbie, where are your manners aren't you going to introduce us?"

Debbie sighed. "Please give me a chance to take off my jacket. Len – this is Mary, she started on Tuesday."

"Hello sweetheart," Len offered his warm welcome and continued, "let me introduce you to the other reprobates. Only joking, there're not that bad when you get to know them. But saying that, when you get to know them, you won't want to meet them again."

"Hurry up Len, we'll fade away with thirst at this rate." His colleague finished the last drop of lager in his pint glass.

"Mary, sweetheart. This is Frank who thinks he is in the desert. He should be in the desert with those looks – makes a camel look attractive. And this is Colin, be careful of him, he can be a bit too friendly. But don't worry he won't be staying long. He has to get back to his Mrs. We've lost count of how many kids he has, and he's not too sure either. Here's Pete. Where's Chris gone?"

"He's in the little boy's room," Colin replied. "Mick's at the bar. I'll let him know the ladies have arrived. What do you want?"

"Dry Martini and lemonade," Debbie replied.

"I'll have the same, thank you." I called out but could not be heard over the noise. Debbie put two fingers in the air to gesture the request for two martinis.

"I will have to record that type of bad behaviour in your HR record. Can't have my staff sticking two fingers in the air." Mr Reed squeezed past Debbie. The pub was crowded but that level of closeness was not necessary. He did not see me at first but then straightened his frame and moved away from Debbie. "Hello Mary. I see Debbie is leading you astray. Would you like a drink?"

"No thank you, Mr Reed. Sorry. I mean Chris," I stuttered. "Mick is buying the drinks."

Mr Reed turned to Debbie, "I didn't know Mick was coming tonight, I thought he was taking his wife out to dinner?"

"No, not our Mick," Debbie replied. "That Mick."

"Alright, darlin.' We'll have to stop meeting like this, people will start to talk." Mick's smile eased my nerves slightly because he was not a complete stranger.

I thanked Mick for the drink and stood next to Debbie.

"No need to run away, darlin,' I don't bite."

"Not yet," Len laughed. "That comes later in the night."

"Be quiet Len," said Frank, "you'll frighten the poor girl off. She's only new."

I felt the comments and looks were patronising which unfortunately triggered the stubborn streak in me and thought, 'I'll show them how I can stand my ground. I'm not a weak, poor girl.' The rebellion against the perceived chauvinistic stereotyping led to self-destructive behaviour which I regret.

The number of customers in the pub lessened gradually. Most men left to return to their family after letting off steam with their colleagues.

"Is that the time?" Mr Reed looked at the large clock above the bar. "Best get off, my son has a rugby match tomorrow morning, and I need all my energy to shout encouragement from the sideline."

"You be careful, Chris, they might mistake you for the new scrum half," Len laughed at his own joke. I kept a straight face and did not dare to even smile.

"Very funny, Len," Mr Reed replied wearily. "Those days have long gone." He tapped Debbie on the arm gently. "I am so tired; I'm going to get a taxi to Waterloo. Do you want a lift. Not wise for you to walk along the embankment on your own."

"Thank you. That is so kind and will be a great relief – my feet are killing me. Will you be alright Mary?"

My words were slurred after drinking on an empty stomach. "Yeah, I'm fine. Hope you have a nice weekend. And the same to you, Chris." My face turned the same shade of dark red as the carpet.

"Good night, Mary, have a nice weekend," Mr Reed ended the working week with a final managerial instruction to the men. "Make sure Mary gets to the station safely."

"Don't worry," proclaimed Mick. "I'll take good care of her, won't I darlin'?"

After Mr Reed and Debbie left the pub, my curious expression led to the revelation. "I know what you are going to ask," Mick sniggered. "The answer is yes. They are more than work colleagues. But best not to say anything. For your sake."

"It's an open secret," Frank moaned. "She can say what she wants."

"Have a day off Frank," Mick replied impatiently. "We all know you fancy Debbie, but I'm afraid the manager is the boss in more ways than one. She's only been here a week. Last thing she needs is to be gossiping about her manager."

"Who's she? The cat's mother?" My catty remark broke the tense exchange.

"Ignore him, sweetheart, "Len said, "He's a roughen. Can't bring him anywhere."

"Sorry darlin' didn't mean to upset you. Let me get you a drink." Mick held out his hand, "come to the bar with me darlin' – show me what you want." He turned to Frank, "what you having?"

"It's alright mate. I'm calling it a night. Had just about enough this week." Frank put his bedraggled suit jacket over his shoulder and shouted out. "Cheers. Be good!"

"He looks so sad," I said.

"Frank will be fine. He still can't get over Debbie refusing to go out with him. He gets so annoyed that he is single, and she is tangled up in being a mistress. Rumour has it that Chris has other close work colleagues, but we won't go there."

"Please don't, "I said. "I don't want to blurt any names by accident if I get flustered."

"I can't wait to get you flustered," Mick whispered in my ear.

"Stop it!" I giggled and nudged his arm. "After that cheeky comment, I'll have a double martini."

"Len, me old mate, got you a whiskey on the rocks," Mick's chirpy tone roused a suspicion in Len, and he winked at his long-time colleague and friend.

"Do you want some sandwiches, sweetheart?" Len asked. "If you don't have something to eat soon, you'll fall over."

"Don't worry darlin' I'll catch you," Mick promoted himself as my protector.

I tucked into the cheese sandwiches which tasted delicious even though the crusts were curled up due to the number of hours they were on display in the glass cabinet located at the end of the bar adjacent to the cigarette machine.

"Do you want one?" Mick put the open cigarette box in front of my face. I was too tired and inebriated to resist the temptation. I had smoked inside the school grounds, by the fire escape. Ashamedly I was stupid enough to think the teachers did not know what was going on – anyone could smell the smoke from a mile off. Ten teenage girls smoking and coughing loudly could not be hidden. The exit doors were fireproof but not soundproof. I nearly choked after taking a couple of puffs of the cigarette from the Marlborough Red packet.

"You alright darlin'?" Mick seemed genuinely concerned.

"What's he doin' to you sweetheart?" Len asked. "You look done in. Do you want me to get you a taxi?"

My stubborn streak surfaced again. "No thank you. I'm fine. I'm still fit and young unlike some around here." I looked at Mick with an alluring smile. My guard was down.

"Now we're getting to the nitty gritty. That was completely ageist and completely true," he laughed. "This old man needs a bar stool right now."

"Would you like a blanket?" I chortled.

"Cheeky." Mick tugged at my arm gently and I stumbled against his leg. "You can lean on me, darlin'," he said and looked at Len. "Time for a song, sir, don't you think?"

Len pretended to warm up with different notes and started singing out of tune but with feeling, "*if you were the only girl in the world and I was the only boy…*"

"Please stop, mate. You'll get us kicked out!" Mick put out his cigarette and cleared his throat. Let the maestro lead,

"Treat me like a fool. Treat me mean and cruel but love me. Break my faithful heart. Tear it all apart but love me. Well, if you ever go. Darling, I'll be oh so lonely. I'll be sad and blue, crying over you, dear only."

"Come on gentleman," said the landlady as she collected the glasses and empty plate. "Last orders and that's your last song, I'm afraid."

"But, Trisha, sweetheart," Len protested lightly, "you love our singing. We're loyal customers. Surely one more song before we go?"

"No more songs, Len. We don't have a licence for concerts or howling." Trisha, the long-suffering landlady, quipped as she started the arduous job of cleaning up after the usual office workers who were filled with frustration about their lives.

I did not notice Mick's hand around my waist whilst I expressed my surprise at how well he held a tune. Or did I willingly participate in this inappropriate intimacy? I wanted to show him that he could not out drink me nor shock me.

"Come on then darlin,' time to get you back to the station," Mick stood up and helped me put on my jacket. "You getting a taxi Len?"

"Yes, sure am. Don't think my old weary legs can hold me up for much longer. I say good night sweetheart but am not allowed to sing it, "Len laughed and leaned over to give me a quick peck on the cheek. "Hope you'll come join us oldies again soon."

"Speak for yourself," Mick retorted. "Give us a bell tomorrow – make sure you're alright?"

Len staggered out of The Ship and Compass, an old-fashioned pub located in a cobbled street, close to Charing Cross rail station, and hailed a black Taxi.

"That'll be an expensive end to the evening for Len?" I enquired.

"Don't worry about Len, darlin, he doesn't live far from here and has got more money than any of us. He doesn't need to work. As you probably noticed he is over retirement age but hates being home on his own after his wife died. He enjoys the banter and gossip in the office and showing off his new suits. So many different stories to tell about him, but we'll save that for another date – yeah?"

I nodded in agreement and in a confused state, was not sure if he meant another day. Surely, he was not asking me out on a date. Such a big difference in age and lives. Mick teased me about my high heels as I tripped on the kerb, and I told him he needs to get a new stylist. The mixture of a floral-patterned tie and a pin stripe shirt is a bit like looking down a kaleidoscope.

"You're lucky I'm not wearing my Hawaiian shirt," Mick smiled and then whispered, "I'm a lucky old man, meeting you." He leaned over and kissed me softly. I was incredibly confused and excited and in disbelief at what had happened during the last week. "You're not that old," I said slowly and brushed the side of his left cheek with my fingers."

"You better go darlin, make sure you don't miss the last train. Take care and I'll see you next week."

I walked towards the entrance of Charing Cross station and then turned to look at Mick walking quickly towards the Embankment underground station. For a fleeting moment, I hoped he would ask me to telephone him tomorrow like he had with Len but soon realised that was a naïve expectation. He had known Len for years.

Mum was not pleased, to put it mildly, about the Friday night drinking club albeit with work colleagues. I did not elaborate on how the group of colleagues thinned out leaving Len, Mick, and me to enjoy the last couple of hours in the traditional old pub with cigarette burns in the patterned carpet. It was not a costly outing because Len bought most of the drinks and food. Mick seemed to be working with a tighter budget but even so would only let me buy one round of drinks, after our colleagues had left. Sometimes Debbie stayed with us which made me feel more comfortable. Mr Reed usually left about 8 p.m. and could not always offer Debbie a lift in a taxi.

Time spent with Mick was erratic and fleeting. Usually, our only time together was in the pub on Friday evenings. After an exchange of kisses in the shadows, I would scramble on the train with other people equally inebriated. When I got off the train, the fear took over, once the late-night commuters started to thin out or were collected by friends in cars. The walk home seemed to last an eternity. I kept to the main roads which made the walk slightly longer but could not face taking the short cut through an alley. How I walked at that speed in heels I still do not understand. There were no speedy boots nor rucksack and no bottle of water which is incomprehensible. How did I manage? It is like another world or dare I say another planet.

What possessed me to be so reckless. Maybe I was annoyed and envious that mum and dad were too interested and worried about Edie's education. If I tried to talk to Edie about Mick, she would have laughed at me and told me in no uncertain fashion to get friends my own age. In fact, she would have drummed home again that I did not have friends and should start thinking about the reason why, before allowing a man to use me, no matter their age. I am not sure if I was secretly hoping to get pregnant? I knew mum worried about me although she did not show it all the time, so it was selfish to put her through those moments of angst. No mobile phones in those days to send travel updates. Dad tried to approach the subject but that was not a strong element of his character - a fascinating concept bearing in mind his outstanding advocacy skills as a barrister. I could wrap him around my finger and shamefully exploited it, but did not get away with everything especially when mum and dad joined forces. Edie told me to stop being selfish and I exploded into a tirade about the so called 'sleepovers' with her friends. I yelled, "it's lucky you have loyal friends, but lying is lying. There are not white lies for you and black ones for me."

If dad had been home or not had a long lunch with clients, he would have given me a lift from the station. It was an incredibly busy time in his career, and he was away from home for lengthy periods of time. I missed him and supposed hoped he would return more if he thought I was getting into trouble. Mum gave me money for taxis, but I used the money to buy cigarettes which was foolish. Mum spent an inordinate amount of time caring for Grandma and Grandpa although they could afford private care. Mum's parents died in accident when she was twenty-nine therefore her in-laws filled a gap in her life. So, maybe what I did was a cry for help but there is no doubt it included a rebellious, "*nothing will happen to me*" attitude. It was stupid and naïve, and no doubt damaged me. To put it in perspective, it could have been far worse, but in retrospect I should have walked away – straight away, without turning back.

When I moved to the Policy Payments department, Mick worked on the same floor which was thrilling and awkward in equal measure. The gossip had spread like wildfire as is par for the course in an office environment. It is dreadful to consider that I thrived on being the hot topic of discussion albeit covered in controversy. Again, a type of rebellion against the acceptable standard of behaviour amongst work colleagues. Eventually, Mick told me he was married which was not that much of a shock. He promised he had filed for divorce, and he had not been unfaithful before, which was not true. I could say that I fell for it, 'hook, line and sinker' however I instinctively knew something was not right – this was not a box standard start of a relationship. No exchange of telephone numbers, no going out on a Saturday evening and no going to lunch together in the staff restaurant.

I cannot recall the exact moment the decision was made to stay overnight in Len's flat. It was inevitable the entanglement would lead to this clandestine destination. Len supported us on the surface but there was no doubt he participated and even fuelled the gossip in the office. In February 1980, Len treated us to an evening at Ronnie Scott's Night Club which was a fantastic experience and conveniently close to his flat. Mick looked melancholy even after a few glasses of whiskey on the rocks, and even the magnificent music could not hide his distant thoughts. He shrugged off reality knocking at the door and sang, quietly, in harmony with the band. Our last night together was our best time together so it was a consolation to end on a happy note, but nothing could detract from the sordid situation. I was addicted to the forbidden fruit, and he was revelling in the boost for his ego. He had snatched the youngest girl in the office.

Eric Nadler, my director was fully aware of the situation. His secretary kept him up to date with the details. Thankfully, Eric was fuming at Mick rather than me. It did not mean I escaped scrutiny, but my attitude to working long hours and taking on extra tasks earned brownie points and most likely saved me from losing my job. Rumour had it that Eric waited for a stag night which he knew would be attended by the men of the Friday Night Drinking Club, before he made his decisive move to end the affair cold in its tracks. During the evening, Eric confronted Mick in front of a stunned crowd, and shared details of the times he had spent with me. Then proclaimed that Mick never had any intention of getting a divorce because his wife was ill and needed his financial support. Reference was made to his previous mistresses, but Eric forcibly reminded everyone that this time it involved a sixteen-year-old girl who he had manipulated from her first week in the company. Not surprising there were no more meetings with Mick. I continued attending the Friday Night Drinking Club for a few weeks to stubbornly show that I could be there without him. Mick did not return to the drinks at The Ship & Compass – he had endured a public telling off and his pride was hurt. He met Len in another pub and only let a select few know the dates. I was excluded from the invitation. I cried a lot and worked a lot more hours. Hiding at work did not stop me feeling sad – it was a distraction.

My team in Policy Payments went out to Covent Garden to celebrate birthdays and other occasions. The first time I joined them; my handbag was stolen. The Police could not understand how or why my handbag was taken from under a pile of coats and other bags. They asked if I had suspicions about any of my colleagues and explained how they could arrange for them to be interviewed. I refused to believe that my, so-called, friends at work would do such a thing. The motivation may not have been to take money but pay back for going out with a married man.

Eric knew he had to get me moved from Policy Payments but did not want it to appear to be due to misconduct on my part. He placed the blame at Mick's feet and placed a note on his HR record. Future promotion opportunities passed him by. Mr Reed also openly supported me. He most definitely did not want the spotlight to be moved to him and Debbie. They both left the Friday Night Drinking Club.

***

Vacancies were advertised in the Group Department, which was located off the Haymarket, next to Her Majesty's Theatre. Eric invited me into his office for an informal chat about how I was settling into the department, my holiday plans and family. He showed me the notification of the vacancies and said, "hot off the press." You have great potential, Mary, do not miss this opportunity. I look upon you as one of the shining stars."

I was ecstatic to be placed in the same category as Simon and Julia – the two cool characters in the department. We all wished they would get together, but it never moved past exquisite flirting which we revelled in. Quite simply Simon was determined to marry his fiancé, and Julia was determined to remain single. Oh, how I wanted to be Julia, but my figure could not fit into her extraordinarily tight pencil skirts nor the starched blouses with turned up collars, and my round face could not wear the short blonde hair cropped into the nap of her neck. I had short dark hair and a pear-shaped figure which I was determined to trim, and was sure the cigarettes would reduce my appetite. Unfortunately, the Marlborough reds prompted a terrible cough. So, I moved to the brand, *Rothmans – King Size.*

"Take a couple of days to think about it. I can have a discussion with Sue to see how we can fast track your promotion." Eric's words were most welcome but at the same time troubling. I thought, 'what has happened to instigate such a quick change?' And 'why is no one else on my grade being offered this opportunity?' Simon and Julia were already higher grades, and they considered applying for the more senior roles in the Group Department which was expanding rapidly.

The manager of the Group Department, John Kindon, asked searching questions about my understanding of Life Assurance and Insurance products, the role of Brokers and my intention to enrol in college to take the ACII (The Associateship of the Chartered Insurance Institute) exams. The interview lasted forty minutes. I was given a background about the department and the plans for the new year. The discussion ended on a lighter note when he asked if I was looking forward to Christmas. "I am afraid my team get a little too enthusiastic with their celebrations, but they are hardworking and could not ask for a better group, excuse the pun." I laughed politely and followed him towards the exit. Curiosity got the better of some members of staff and their exaggerated staring made me feel even more awkward. I waved goodbye to the manager which was entirely inappropriate however when I turned to escape from my embarrassment, one person caught my eye. The warmth of his blue eyes showed a genuine interest, and he nodded gently, and I reciprocated. My first interaction with Neil Bach was subtle but spiralled into my core and intertwined into each particle of my psyche.

***

CHAPTER 4

"How did you manage to wangle tickets for the Royal Enclosure?" Jo shrieked down the telephone.

My niece was dismayed at how I had obtained tickets for Ladies Day at Royal Ascot on Thursday 22 June. Her level of surprise matched my level of nerves before attending such a prestigious event.

"So, is this the regular, caring telephone call to your Aunty?" I replied. "Are you really interested or just suffering from your latest bout of FOMO?"

"I'm sorry I called you now," Jo retorted. "Just curious."

"You know what curiosity did to the cat, "I teased my niece and held the handset away from my ear in anticipation of the rant.

"You are so boringly predictable," Jo groaned. "For the record I do not want to go to a place where I am told what to wear including those preposterous hats. Anyway, I have tickets to a bigger and better event."

I interrupted her announcement and asked, "Don't tell me. Henley Royal Regatta?"

"You are being deliberately annoying now," she snapped. "Do you want to know? Or do you want to go back to your knitting?"

"Sorry," I said sheepishly. "I'm all ears."

"At last," she said. "Glastonbury Festival. Can't wait."

"Are you going with Chen?" I asked. The hesitant response set off low pitched alarm bells at this stage. 'There could be a thousand and one reasons why he could not go.' I thought. 'Or could be just one reason – the final curtain call?'

"His super busy. Not sure yet. I was thinking of asking Seonaid?" Jo was testing the water about asking her niece.

"Don't think your brother would like his daughter stuck in mud amidst a bunch of hippies," I replied with an added subtext. "Am I allowed to say hippy in 2023?"

"Say what you want," Jo quipped. "I'm not recording our conversation. She'll probably be playing cricket or practising in the nets or whatever you call it. I blame granddad for talking her into being a sports fan."

"Seonaid is as stubborn as you, well almost. No one talks her into anything," I reminded Jo that she did not have exclusive rights to the share of stubbornness in the family. "I read in the newspaper that Elton John is going to be there?"

"A newspaper?" Jo giggled mockingly. "Yes, Elton John is the headline act. I'm worried he's a bit too old, about the same age as you, isn't he?"

"How rude!" I laughed and corrected my niece's calculation. "He was born in 1947 not 1963 as you well know. He's still a great performer. One of my favourite songs is Star Man."

Jo tutted, "It's Rocket Man. You'd be a great asset to a fan club. Starman was by David Bowie."

"I'll have you know; I was a great member of The Bay City Roller Fan Club." I proudly protested. "I knew all their songs – actually, all the lyrics of the songs."

"Really?" Jo yawned. "Aldo said Rick Astley is due to be there on Saturday. Another golden oldie. Bet you liked his songs, Aunty?"

"Certainly did." I replied. "You must have heard of *'Never Gonna Give You Up'?*"

"Think so?" Jo sounded perplexed. "How does it go? On second thoughts. I'll Google it. My ears can't cope with your dulcet tones."

I sugar-coated my concern about Aldo with a playful question. "Will you be glamping? Aldo must have a lot of contacts to get you into the VIP area

"Don't be silly." Jo replied. "Aldo is having fantastic success in Edinburgh. We keep in contact by WhatsApp which means text in your world." Jo gave an explanation reluctantly with a punch line. "You can pass the news update onto mum. Am sure she wants to know but gets you to do the dirty work."

"She worries about you," I said and immediately realised I walked straight into the trap.

"Funny way of showing it," Jo snapped. "Leaving your daughter for a fancy man in Italy is not a sign of responsible parenting in my books."

I delivered my rebuttal with a sharp sarcastic tone, "I agree he is handsome, wouldn't say fancy, mind you. But a key factor – he is your mum's husband and one extremely vital ridge on the key – to unlock the conundrum, is that he loves your mother unconditionally. Rare blessing to find during our fleeting time in this domain. Please do not lose sight of the facts."

"Alright. If you say so," Jo sulked. "I must go now. Cosimo needs my help with the change in scenery and costumes. And there's absolutely no point talking to you when you go into officialdom mode. Before I forget, you didn't answer my question; who gave you tickets to Royal Ascot? Go on spill the beans. Do you have a new fancy man like mum?"

"No!" I replied more abruptly than intended. "Miss Drake gave me the tickets. One of her clients could not go and she offered them to me."

"She's too scary," Jo's voice trembled for dramatic affect. "Did she use one of her spells to stop the client going?"

"Stop it, Jo," I reprimanded my niece. "You know how dedicated Miss Drake is to her shop. There is no way she is going to close for one day to watch horseracing, even if members of the Royal Family are there."

"Still think she is strange," Jo said, "but lift my hat off to her for still working so hard at her age. How old is she now? Got to be about ninety, surely?"

"No. Think she is eighty this year," I replied. "She is kindly adjusting my dress and even found a hat by Philip Treacy, in her Aladdin's cave, that I can borrow. Wow!"

"Will you turn into a pumpkin if you do not return it by midnight?" Jo smirked.

"You can mock her, but she could help with the theatrical costumes," I said. "You are missing out on a real traditional talent. The fast fashion factories do not have these skills. I am sure Cosimo would be delighted with your blue sky thinking."

"You've been eating too much chocolate again, Aunty," Jo chortled. "Talking of Cosimo, I need to go, right now. Lovely talking to you, Aunty, about an eclectic mixture of topics as usual. Take care and I'll call you again soon."

"Thank you, Jo. Look after yourself," I replied. "You know where I am if you need anything."

Miss Ely Drake is the manager of Drying Days & Sewing Streams – the local dry cleaners. The shop sign in Italic Calligraphy, hangs from the arch above the traditional front door made of dark brown solid hardwood, with thick circular patterned (bullseye) glass encased in square panels, on the top half, and a cat flap masterfully carved into the bottom left corner; close to the stone step on which stands a vintage, Victorian style, cast iron, boot scraper. A grand entrance into the intricate creativity and dedication to delivering excellent customer service with an eye for detail and an ear to listen to the individual need of each customer. Wesley, the silver-grey, old male cat rarely uses the cat flap now. He times his adventures outside very well and the onslaught of the increased volume of traffic encourages him to stay home for longer. The occasional stray or opportunistic cat enters through the cat flap cautiously but does not get far. Although Wesley is of a certain age, he still gives out a mighty blow with his south paw.

Miss Drake is an eccentric character and has a sixth sense. Her first name is rarely used or known. She prefers the mystery and aloofness. She offers excellent cleaning service and needlework repairs. An exquisite seamstress. Miss Drake knew mum and Grandma and they shared a respectful professional friendship with a warm underlay. She has an old-fashioned hand operated Singer – sewing machine in the window of her small shop in Comatt Mews, close to the rail station, just off the High Street. A family business for decades. She inherited her skills and business from her father and Grandfather who was a Jewish refugee. She is a widow but does not want to close the shop. Her children keep in minimal contact: they are not interested in the business but are extremely interested in the real estate. In recent years they have had more conversations with Tarquin than their mother. He is only too happy to explore the potential for a sale to a property developer who would snap up the chance of the prime site. My niece is reluctant to go to see Miss Drake about the creation or repair of costumes for theatrical productions. Jo says she is like a witch. An unkind comment but it represents the feeling of some in the area. I have doubts whether Cosimo, the Director of production, would accept and respect Miss Drake, due to her creative expertise, which is not typically found in central London. Too many temporary staff out to make a quick profit and move swiftly onto the next money-making scheme. Cosimo would not tolerate being challenged. Miss Drake would not tolerate second best or a quick fix just to get the job done. In her line of thought, it is either perfection or pointless. There is no, "it'll do" attitude in Miss Drake's mind.

Miss Drake does not recognise the word 'retire' and will only stop when her health stops. Her resilience is inspirational and overwhelming in equal measure.

Tarquin used to get his designer suits and shirts cleaned in 'Drying Days & Sewing Streams.' Miss Drake made sure each button was sewn on tightly and there was not one thread out of place. The clothes were stored carefully in a branded, full length zip closure, canvas suit cover. She did not use the clear plastic covers; or bags, as she called them. Miss Drake made an extra special effort when Tarquin was preparing for Royal Ascot and the Henley Royal Regatta. Invites and complimentary tickets were readily available when business was booming, and commission was culminating in large bonuses. However, change cuts through our lives in different slices. Tarquin suffers immensely from FOMO (fear of missing out). The events dried up therefore the visits to Miss Drake reduced and came to a halt when he found pins left in his clothes which were strategically hidden. They gave an uncomfortable pointed message about his cheating on Edie when she had two children.

***

Edie Crowmere – Gale (nee Danrich), my sister, started work in a library two months after her 18th birthday. Mum said, "she needs a couple of months to rest after the success in her 'A' levels." I did not understand what she was resting from, and Edie did not understand why anyone would refer to her grades as a success. In her view, only straight A* grades are worthy of a celebration. I truly think the exam results knocked her confidence sideways: an unusual concept to witness never mind understand. The fact that Tyrone York, the coolest boy in the sixth form, ended their tentative relationship one week before the exams in front of their friends in the common room did not help. One could say it was nerves affecting his decision-making process or if we open the door to reality – he was infecting Edie with negative thinking to impact her ability to concentrate. Why? With my cynical head on the reason was envy because in the mock exams Edie was the only student to achieve straight A* results and that was a podium he wanted to stand on alone. Is this an unfair assessment on my part? Might be. There was also the minor factor that Edie refused to spend an evening studying with him which was code for sleeping with him, and his ego was damaged. Tyrone had a 100% score card up until that point. Edie did not tell me the entire story, so I put the snippets of information from mum and Susie Beatty, our hairdresser, together. Primrose Pensel – one of Edie's closest school friends, shared how Tyrone, "dumped" Edie. Primrose did not usually speak to me very much; however, went out of her way to tell me the news whilst waiting for Edie to return from the hairdresser. Edie's friendship with Primrose did not last much longer, because Tyrone asked Primrose to his 18th birthday party, as his date, which was a prestigious position in the social hierarchy. Tyrone and Primrose got engaged six months later but the relationship did not have longevity. Tyrone went on a gap year to Australia and eventually formalised his emigration to the land down under, where the life close to Manly was too good to miss. His wealthy parents funded the move and accommodation close to the beautiful beach. Primrose was left holding their baby without payment of child maintenance.

***

The library in Greenwich provided solace and quietude for Edie after a tumultuous period for her emotions. Mum and Grandma were confounded by Edie's career choice and aired their disapproval. Dad and Grandpa were more empathetic which was quite a role reversal. However, they unanimously reached the conclusion – it was just a bump in the road. Edie would pick herself up and the serenity of the library provided the opportunity to pursue her interest in history and art. There was an eclectic and extensive range of books and a variety of art exhibitions in the area. The repetitive tasks were a distraction for Edie, and she enjoyed going to the antique shops. The expanse of Greenwich Park freed up the mind and helped let loose the anxiety. Edie was enchanted by the visits to the Old Royal Naval College, especially the Painted Hall.

The Council promoted initiatives to attract more members of the community and tourists to visit the library even though the exterior was crumbling and in need of renovation. Evening events including authors and artists proved to be a success. Edie organised the table displays for the budding authors who were filled with nervous energy. Their inaugural book signings were overwhelming even if they only had ten customers. The established authors gave talks and spent longer signing their books to a sell-out audience. Art workshops were popular especially during school holidays. The lectures by an art historian fascinated Edie and the attendees. Mum worried about the late evenings but at the same time sincerely hoped Edie would meet scholars to re-ignite her interest to go to university and Grandma fantasised about Edie meeting an artist – the next *Joseph Mallord William Turner.* Grandma admired immensely the painting, *The Fighting Temeraire Tugged to Her Last Berth to Be Broken Up,* and had a print, protected in a hand-crafted wooden frame, in the living room above the fireplace.

One artist extended an invitation to Edie to consider applying for a role in The Victoria & Albert Museum in Kensington. Edie proclaimed with glee that she had been head hunted. Mum and dad congratulated her, but I wondered if there was a hint of romance in the air when I saw the sparkle in her eyes. Interviews do not usually generate that much excitement. Grandma was over the moon when Edie announced she had been offered the role a research assistant in The National Art Library. Our family thought the apprenticeship scheme would surely, lead to a connection with a mature, sincere man gifted with an artistry to secure their future.

Fate can flaw dreams in a blink of an eye or in this case a wink of Tarquin Crowmere – Gale's eye.

Dale Estate Agents organised an evening event at the V&A Museum to celebrate their 10th anniversary on the High Street and a record-breaking year for commission. Edie and her work colleagues volunteered to help the event manager and thought it would be fun to mix with a different clientele for a few hours. Members of the Executive Board of the museum anticipated an agreement for future corporate partnership with Dale Estate Agents bearing in mind their wealth which was on shameless display that evening. Edie was drunk on champagne and chat up lines. Tarquin diverted her attention from artistic talent to absolute twaddle. Although he was a prize-winning author of verbal fiction.

Mum and dad's aspiration for their daughter was extinguished by a salesman.

Grandma was delighted when she first heard the name Tarquin, but her high hopes sunk to the depths of despair when the truth surfaced.

Tarquin seemed to be in a hurry to get married. Edie was flattered by the attention and blinded by the blaze of over exaggerated signs of affection especially when out with her friends who were rapidly distancing themselves from her strange behaviour. Edie did not telephone them as promised which was most unlike her. Her style of clothes changed as well as her hairstyle. Susie Beatty asked me why Edie had not made an appointment for a while. "She's found someone new, hasn't she?" Susie laughed. "Break it to me gently."

"She's found someone new alright," I said. "And only wish she would break it off with him."

The wedding in September 1981 was not a big occasion due to the lack of attendance from Tarquin's family. His work colleagues flitted in and out between viewings. "Can't miss out on a sale, can we lads?" This particular line in the groom's speech fell flat. Dad forced a smile to try to be polite and mum just nodded her head to the side and bit her lip. The reception in the Bromley Court Hotel was frugal. Tarquin insisted on a buffet. "More chance to mingle" he said. Dad made a polite and brief speech. Offering congratulations to the newlyweds and commenting how beautiful his daughter looked and how deeply beautiful she is as a person. Although I cringed inside with envy, my eyes filled with tears – not with joy but with fear. What had Edie got herself into? Tarquin beguiled her with empty promises and falsified empathy in respect of Tyrone. Regrettably, Edie let Tarquin into the vaults of her pain in pursuit of an open and honest marriage vow. An admirable aim however in the wrong hands, each intimate detail of how Tyrone betrayed her, formed a powerful weapon in the armoury of coercive behaviour. In this case scenario Tarquin not only had an armoury but also a set target i.e. to prove to his relatives he could win over a beautiful and intelligent wife and would be more financially successful than them. The alarm bells rang louder when we found out that Edie had not met Tarquin's parents nor spoke to them. The entire situation was awkward. Grandma clung to the hope his heritage would keep him in good stead, and he would eventually open an independent Estate Agent more suited to an upper-class clientele. When our faces fell, Grandma claimed, "He could start a successful family business which will be a magnificent inheritance for their children."

***

Tarquin, Sebastian, Jonathan, Rowland, Crowmere–Gale, my sister's first husband, was born in 1955 in East Grinstead in Kent. Tarquin is related to George Rikes – the main partner of RH & RW CLYTON in 1974. He Retired in 2012. The company is a leading independent property consultancy offering an extensive range of services including residential estate agent. The roots of the property business date back to 1743. The company has an expert team based in East Grinstead and Petworth. Tarquin's father put him under a lot of pressure to join the company however he could not meet the standard of the other professionals and tension between father and son made him leave to work in central London. Tarquin wanted to and needed to prove a point and earn more commission. He thought "surely the deals with HNWI (High-Net-Worth Individuals) would leave the results of RH & RW CLYTON in the shade?" Tarquin's ego and narcissistic traits blinkered his observance of the potential potholes and diversions in the road to the enviable success which he craved.

***

Edie and Tarquin's first child, Sebastian Charles, arrived on Saturday 14th November 1981. Tarquin was conveniently enjoying a fishing weekend with friends. We never got to find out who he was with, but he told us about each fish he caught in detail. There were no mobiles in those days, and the land line number he left with Edie did not connect. He told us that he spent most of the time on the riverbank therefore a message would not have reached him. The pieces of the puzzle did not add up because Tarquin did not like to be too far away from the next sale. One of his friends must have been keeping in contact with someone at the Estate Agent office. How the hotline was managed remains a mystery.

We had anticipated Edie starting University at the age of twenty-one. Instead, she was taking shaky steps on the path to being a full-time single mum. I say single because Tarquin worked hard and played hard to influence and find more deals. "How else am I going to afford to pay for my son to go to Oxford?" he would boast loudly. My rebellious mode rose to the surface sometimes, especially after another sleepless night trying to help care for Sebastian so Edie could get a few hours' sleep and snapped back, "your son needs time with you not your money!"

Edie and Tarquin's second child, Joanna Tabitha, arrived on 4th May 1988. A longer gap in years between the two siblings than Edie anticipated and had wanted. Tarquin's work schedule and networking events filled his calendar and his mind. Tarquin dropped suggestions into the rare conversations he had with his wife e.g. "you and Sebastian make a great team. Made for each other – from a fine gene pool. You know what they say, two's company, three's a crowd." Edie did not buckle to these persuasive and invasive comments. Unfortunately, Edie seduced Tarquin with extra glasses of whiskey and intense flattery. Hoping beyond imagination she would win her husband back from work commitments and intimate networking evenings, with a new baby.

Tarquin was in the hospital whilst Edie endured an extremely lengthy and excruciatingly painful delivery. The hospital telephoned mum because the consultant was becoming increasingly concerned for the wellbeing of Edie. A recommendation was made for Edie to have a caesarean, but Tarquin insisted she would be fine. The long recovery time after the operation would be an inconvenience. Edie wanted her mum by her side and told dad and me to "GET OUT!" which was perfectly understandable in the circumstances. Dad used his portfolio of contacts to arrange for Edie to be moved to a private suite as soon as practical after the birth and for a private gynaecologist to assess the extent of the physical trauma. I thanked the midwife sitting in the office for their hard work. She said Edie would have been less stressed and there may have been fewer issues if she had been on her own with the midwife. My puzzled expression emanating from my tired facial features prompted the midwife to say, "I'm sorry, I do not mean to interfere, but we could hear the arguments in the corridor from your sister's room. At one point, I went to check on your sister and requested your brother-in-law leave to get a cup of coffee."

I did not really comprehend the seriousness of the commentary from the midwife and replied flippantly, "I'm sure you are used to the mothers shouting at their husbands? I don't blame them – I'd be shouting and throwing things at my husband, if I had one."

"Please excuse me for saying," she replied. "It is important to share our concerns. Your sister's husband was shouting at her. He kept repeating, '*I haven't got time for this!*' She was in floods of tears when I went to see her. That is the main reason I asked him to leave to give your sister a break. He said he couldn't get through to you or your mum."

"We didn't get any calls?" I whispered slowly and lost my balance.

"I'm sorry," the midwife replied. "We thought he would keep trying to contact you. We assumed you must have been out for the day."

"No. We were in all day. Even dad had a day off." I mumbled in a daze and could not digest what was happening.

The midwife reached out to touch my arm, "your sister has your mum with her now. Let them be together for a while. If Edie can calm down, even slightly, it should ease the final stages."

"Yes, of course," I smiled politely and gratefully. "Edie has already made it abundantly clear she does not want me or dad anywhere near her. I'll get some tea and food for mum and then pop out to buy extra toiletries for them both and not forgetting baby."

The private gynaecologist's diagnosis delivered the news that it would be highly unlikely for Edie to have any more children. The internal damage, partially caused by the delays and disruption in the delivery suite, is inoperable. A bleak prospect for an otherwise fit and healthy twenty-eight-year-old. However, she did not have the strength nor the support from her husband to manage any more children. The consensus in the family was that Tarquin was not committed

73

to the wedding vows nor his family. I held onto hope that Edie would eventually meet someone who will love her unconditionally. He would need to be empathetic and accept that they would not have children. *"There are plenty of single fathers out there."* I thought. *"One of them must have solid scruples?"* But this was not the time for match making. The family did everything possible to support Edie who was extremely grateful but sometimes pushed back especially when she thought mum labelled her as a victim. Edie's inner strength strained under the weight of Tarquin's narcissistic tendencies, and lack of sleep. Baby, Joanna Tabitha, had a good set of lungs which she aired most of the night. I spent many hours walking the floor, *'doing the magic'* – Edie's description of how I bounced up and down. In fact, it looked like an awkward attempt at the Samba; one dance that I did not master when at the dancing school and it showed. Unfortunately, Jo demanded a turn on the dance floor before going to sleep. When I played the cassettes of the songs 'Only You' by Yazoo and 'Lullaby of Broadway' by Doris Day, Jo relaxed and even seemed to move her arms in time to the beat. Tarquin complained profusely when he was at home. "Turn that racket off!" His harsh tone unsettled Jo and she screamed.

Sebastian was, mostly, not perturbed by his new housemate. Although during one of Jo's extended *screamathon*s, Sebastian did ask, "when is she going back to the hospital?" Grandma and Grandpa were pleased to look after Sebastian, and he revelled on the sole attention but thankfully it did not turn him into a spoilt brat. In fact, the time invested by grandma and grandpa led him to be studious and successful and settled in his own skin. Jo was caught in a fraught atmosphere and her behaviour reflected the tension. Tarquin did not like mum and dad visiting even when he was not at home which was most nights. The lid on the pressure cooker came off when Edie asked, "who was Kamlai Peech?" The Christmas card from Kamlai was addressed only to Tarquin and inside the message read, "To my Gladiator, fighting to the end to deliver the best deal in town. Thank you, Tarquin. Warm wishes from Kamlai xx"

"Don't panic!" Tarquin's patronising reply continued, "she's a potential buyer. The search for her dream home has taken a lot of my time and skilled negotiation, so don't want you phoning the office or trying to contact her. Do you understand?"

"I don't want to talk to her," Edie replied. "Just trying to get my head around the meaning of the words in her Christmas card and why wasn't this handed into the office?"

"Don't worry your pretty head!" Tarquin's sarcastic tone tormented Edie but she did not have the energy to retaliate. "Crucial that I get the commission before the end of the year. Must surpass my target and get top Agent award. Beating Quenton is a bonus. Can't wait to wipe that smug smile off his face."

Kamlai Peech evolved into Tarquin's second wife. Their affair started a year after Jo was born. Tarquin couldn't stand the noise nor the smell of nappies and interfering in-laws, so his escape route included a woman, nearly eighteen years younger. She is petite and has porcelain skin but has a sharp and direct intent to get what she wants. Kamlai inherited her mother's survival instinct – born into poverty in Thailand but escaped by marrying a British bank manager. Kamlai's father left his first wife for a younger model – his choice of words accurately reflected his contempt for commitment. The name Kamlai means '*bracelet.*' Jo says the accurate description is handcuffs.

Tarquin eventually left the family home in 1993 when Sebastian was twelve and Jo was five. Both children starting new schools and in need of the united support from their parents. Edie's sadness was overridden by relief which haunted her with guilt, because her children had to separate from the relationship with their father. She tried to take on the joint role of a mother and father and invented new stories a.k.a. excuses to cover Tarquin's absence each time there was a meeting with a teacher. The yummy mummies at the school gates overlooked Edie because she did not wear the fashionable outfits with designer bags and her social life was not as exciting and busy as their out-of-school timetable. When Jo first met her friend Araminta Peabody who she called Minty, she wanted to go back to her home for each evening for tea. Edie felt the blow of rejection and rebellion and tried to explain that Minty's family needed time and space on their own. "They'll adopt me. I know they will," a seven-year-old Jo proclaimed. Edie was not sure how Jo grasped the concept of adoption, but this was the beginning of the emotional battle with her daughter. When at Minty's home there were no gushing statements about Sebastian and no complaints about Tarquin. There was just the freedom to be a child and share her creative talents with her friend. Minty's parents grew protective over Jo. Edie was extremely grateful but did not want to outsource her parental responsibilities especially when Tarquin thoroughly documented her mistakes and weaknesses but did not have the same enthusiasm in documenting his child maintenance payments nor arranging dates to see his children. Initially Sebastian wanted his dad to watch him play football but eventually became despondent after Tarquin did not turn up as promised. The reason given each time. "Too busy! Can't miss a sale. Never know who knows the buyer. It's all about networking – making good contacts! You'll understand son, when you get a job."

Edie rebuked her estranged husband, "shame you can't keep in contact with your children. But they don't equate to commission, so they are of no real value to you, are they?"

Tarquin used to slam the phone down at this point. He did not have the patience nor interest to waste his time on such trivial matters.

The divorce of Edie and Tarquin was finalised in 1994. Tarquin married his mistress as quickly as possible because she was expecting their first child. The decision was not made based a moral or religious foundation but out of vanity because Kamlai wanted a professional photoshoot as part of the wedding arrangements. An additional cost for Tarquin to worry about and another amount '*borrowed*' from his savings account set aside for his child maintenance payments which were long overdue. Their daughter was born in 1995 and the name selected by her mother is Chailai – a mood-boosting Thai girl name meaning pretty.

Jo says her name sounds like Chihuahua. Tarquin calls her 'Cha Cha-Cha' which infuriates both his daughters in equal measure. The only thing they have in common. Tarquin had no input into the choice of the names for his second family.

The arrival of Tarquin's youngest daughter disrupted his 40th birthday celebrations which annoyed him because each party is an opportunity to meet potential buyers and new employers to fulfil his dream – to be head hunted by a prestigious Estate Agent in Mayfair.

Sebastian and Jo planned to go out with their father to celebrate his birthday. He promised. He cancelled. The trip to the Hard Rock Cafe, standing on the edge of Green Park and Hyde Park was postponed and added to the profusion of empty promises that never materialised. Jo had hoped to persuade her dad to take a detour to a theatre in Shaftesbury

Avenue before going home but that was an ambition put on the back burner for a future date when Jo would direct each step to the stage door.

***

Tarquin and Kamlai's second child, Ignatius, was born in 1997: named after Kamlai's late British father who was intrigued by Sir Arthur Ignatius Conan Doyle: the creator of the fictional character Sherlock Holmes. Kamlai insisted their children did not have middle names. "One name is sufficient." She pronounced with finality. We awaited Jo's commentary and were not disappointed.

"He'll probably turn into the Hound of the Baskervilles." Jo giggled. I thought it was quite funny for a nine-year-old girl but at the same time wondered who introduced her to such a frightening story. Edie said Sebastian's friends tried to scare Jo with images from the film An American Werewolf in London and she started studying stories about hounds or wolves howling. Edie tried to distract her, but intense curiosity took hold, and we all know what curiosity did to the cat. The inevitable nightmares followed for a couple of months and dissipated when mum and dad treated Jo to a ticket to see the hit musical 'Oliver!' at the London Palladium. Jo's shrill of excitement deflated to a grumble when it was announced I was her companion for the outing to this magnificent theatre. "Well, you can't go on your own!" Edie snapped.

***

Tarquin had not anticipated having two young children in primary school at the age of fifty. Sebastian and Jo, aged twenty-four and seventeen respectively, had all but lost contact and interest in their father. Tarquin had to put off his mid-life crisis – his much-anticipated purchase of a Ferrari and a penthouse in Belgravia had to remain on the crumpled bucket list. Tarquin assessed his circumstances and reached the conclusion his young pretty wife is good for business i.e. she attracts attention at corporate events, and he thrived on the envy of his colleagues and directors. He believed the kudos would benefit his much desired and needed promotion. Kamlai retained her role as a house manager. Tarquin preferred her concentrating on their children rather than a wealthy chief executive officer focusing on her attractive qualities. Jo's critique of Kamlai covers a variety of topics, but her loudest complaint is in relation to her unemployed status. "Why doesn't she work and earn a living? Dad might have some money for us now and again if it wasn't funding her lifestyle!" Edie tried to explain to her daughter that having children is the most important and difficult role anyone can take on. "You wait until you have children! Then you'll understand." Edie raised her voice to deliver her warning about the reality of life.

Jo replied in a formidable force, "Yeah, right!" Edie and me sensed Jo did not have a maternal instinct and was not a homemaker like mum or grandma.

Tarquin's youngest daughter, Chailai, is a Beautician. Jo thinks she is a bit of an 'air head' and complains, "she has taken the easy option -working in the beauty business. They don't work long hours and do not have to study or strive for next contract or promotion. Chailai is content with her choice. Flexible working and gets to talk to a lot of people. She wants her dad to buy her a new salon on the High Street. Her mother does not want a beauty parlour in the garden even if it is designed like a Swiss Chalet and most definitely does not want to set up a beauty room in their lovely new and expensive house. Tarquin secured a good deal on the property – called in a favour to get a bigger house but it results him having to work many more hours to repay the person in question. Tarquin refuses to ask his dad for a loan although his parents could easily afford it. He informed his parents about Chailai in a brief note at the bottom of a Christmas card. There was no response nor interest.

Ignatius is a rebel and a complex character. He dropped out of college and cannot keep a job. He is not really interested in anything but wants to travel however does not have the money. Jo says he should join the army and thinks his dad will insist he is a mercenary so he can earn money and get a bonus if successful. Sebastian lets Jo's sharp comments go over his head and keeps a respectful distance from their dad. He tried to help Ignatius, by arranging work experience in a lawyer's office, but he only lasted a week. A lost opportunity and humiliation for Sebastian who does not want to risk his professional reputation on an ungrateful individual, even if the apprentice is his half-brother.

Ignatius, who demands to be called Iggy, is an embarrassment to Tarquin who tells his colleagues his younger son is either studying or on a 'gap' year but is confident he'll make a great Estate Agent one day! Nothing could be further from the truth.

**

Edie's turbulent introduction to motherhood was sad to witness and cut deep into her psyche. Sebastian's steady personality strengthened the bond with his grandad and nan and even more so with his grandpops and gan-gan (great grandparents).

The splinters from the fractious relationship between her parents stuck under Jo's skin and hurt. For some reason, I took on the responsibility of removing the splinters one by one when I could get close enough to Jo which was a rare occurrence.

***

CHAPTER 5

Green tea stains in the cream carpet are difficult to remove. I tried the carpet shampoos and an old toothbrush, but the discoloured patch spread across the space between the armchair and small coffee table. I slumped in the cosy old armchair. The faded floral pattern tucked into each corner. I can still hear mum's words, "it'll last you a lifetime – they don't make them like that anymore," as she donated the item of furniture as a flat warming gift. A cushion purchased from the charity shop bolstered the seat. I looked around the living room of my one-bedroom flat. The wallpaper had aged well for the most part however the black spots of mould by the balcony doors curled up in reaction to the condensation. The small disposable & non spill moisture trap containers are effective but the supply in the hall cupboard has run out. The last time I went to Robert Dyas there was only the lavender scented Krystals in stock. I prefer the smell of damp rather than lavender.

"I really should decorate?" I thought. "Will be more appealing to potential buyers."

The decision to put my flat on the market to test the water was made after Jo insisted, I should at least explore the options. "You'll go old and mouldy sitting there on your own!" Jo's words stung and she would not make a popular life coach, but she has a point.

"What have I got to lose?" I thought.

Asking Tarquin for help was like asking a fox to help refurbish a chicken house but the other Estate Agents baffled me with market predictions and volatility in price. At least with Tarquin I know he is fabricating the entire situation so do not have sift out the facts.

Tarquin jumped at the chance to help. Jo was horrified. "Help?" she chortled. "When does my father help anyone? But he'll help himself to commission!"

I am worn down by the different decisions and doubts, but Tarquin guarantees Dale Estate Agents will sell the property quickly and he will secure the best price.

Within two days of contacting Tarquin, I was notified that two couples were due to be at my flat at 9 a.m. on Saturday morning. I changed the time to 10:30 a.m. and stipulated that this is the earliest time for viewings on a Saturday. My neighbours, albeit distantly polite, work long hours therefore do not want to antagonise them by loud-mouth Estate Agents and squealing excited potential buyers stomping though the shared corridor.

On Saturday 8th July, my thorough cleaning campaign started at 08:00 a.m. Making the bed was the first task. Whoever thought of that saying? I squashed and patted the duvet cover until it looked semi-ironed. Hid my nightdress under the pillow, wiped down the bedside cabinet and moved all the toiletries on top of the chest of drawers into last remaining space in the bottom drawer, and worried that it would get stuck with the overcrowding. The clothes dryers had to be put in the shared hall to remove the trip hazard along with the shopping trolley that I insisted that I did not need, but Edie said it would help carry the laundry during the ongoing saga with the broken washing machine.

"They're trendy, aunty." Jo proclaimed when she delivered the gift on behalf of her mum.

"Oh really," I replied. "We can compare designs on the bags, can't we?" I looked at the lines on her forehead as they creased in disdain. "No? Thought not!" I replied on her behalf.

Making the bathroom look appealing was a challenge. After a quick shower, I wiped the bath but attempts to remove all the scale marks from the taps and shower attachments were not successful. Old tea towels were used to wipe the glass shower door – the mould on the seal stuck fast therefore made it impossible to remove from the base of the door which rested on the side of the bath. I nudged the loose bath panel back into place. The blind was too heavy for the window fitting so I moved it gently upwards to clean the edge of the shelf. I abandoned the attempt to use the dust magnet starter kit because the description and images on the colourful, excellently branded box, did not match the duster in my hands. I used old tights to clean the separate rails of the chrome towel rail in the bathroom. The laundry basket, filled to the brim with dirty dusters and dish cloths and towels, was put in the shared hall. My neighbours were understanding of my plight and lack of adequate space in readiness for a surge of visitors: Tarquin told me he had already lined up a horde of potential buyers. I took his over inflated empty promise with a pinch of salt.

Each cupboard and shelf were packed full of items which we pretend we do not have in our homes. Clear surfaces are crucial, so says the guidelines on the internet, and the instructions from my niece. I am not sure why my niece is so keen on selling my flat – what is her motivation? If I go to live near my sister in Italy, it would be a cheap holiday. I hope she is not expecting money from the sale of the flat because she will be sorely disappointed. Dad set up a trust fund for her but most annoyingly it will be paid on her 40th birthday. If I choose the option to move abroad there will not be much left of the so-called profit after paying fees to the lawyers, removal company and the special '*knockdown fee*' arranged by Tarquin. He used the old trick of starting at a higher percentage fee and knocked off 30% which equated to the standard fee.

If I move to Kenley in Surrey to be closer to Sebastian, the amount required for a deposit is extortionate so there will not be much left in the gift piggy bank for Jo. I also need to consider that Sebastian is a successful lawyer, and his professional skills are broadcast far and wide. There is a real possibility he could be offered a contract abroad although this is highly unlikely until his children, Ewan aged fifteen and Seonaid aged thirteen, have finished their university education. But children are more independent these days so they may have a different view than their Great Aunty Mary. Ewan is studious like his dad. Seonaid is as rebellious as her Aunt Joanna so university may not even be considered. She loves cricket – a skill inherited from her great grandfather (my dad) who was a keen cricket fan and player in his youth. He played for Outwood Cricket Club: Outwood is a village and civil parish in the Tandridge district of the Surrey weald. His parents were extremely proud of their son, Thomas Hugh Gilbert, born in 1932. A lot of thought went into selecting the names – a mindset that infuriates my niece. She gets incredibly frustrated with our obsession for family names and their history. Thomas was a tribute to Thomas Bowley a first-class English cricketer who played for Surry. The roots of the middle name, Hugh, are in the Tandridge churchyard – an ancient yew tree, of a size to indicate it is over 1,500 years old. Gilbert was a tribute to Sir George Gilbert Scott RA (13 July 1811 – 27 March 1878) who was a prolific English Gothic Revival architect; chiefly associated with the design, building and renovation of churches and cathedrals, although he started his career as a leading designer of workhouses. A tenuous link to the Pro Bono work carried out by my dad throughout his career.

My grandpa and my dad were members of the MCC (Marylebone Cricket Club) which they both cherished.

* * *

The professional oven cleaners were due next Friday. I placed a clean tea towel over the handle on the oven door to hide the grease marks inside. At 10:00 a.m. I finished hoovering, pushed the Dyson vacuum cleaner into the back of the hall meter cupboard and made cups of coffee for that warm homely feeling. I do not have an espresso machine. Freshly baked bread is not my forte. Those two tips were crossed off my list for successful viewings. The coffee bags are strong and thankfully masked the abundance of cleaner products used on the kitchen sink to remove the tea stains.

The sound of the buzzer on the intercom rattled around the hall. the booming voice on the other end announced, "Dale Estate Agents! We're here for the ten-thirty viewing." I dashed around the flat to make sure I had not left items of underwear on the radiator wire airers, and the coffee cup was in a strategic position. I opened the door in anticipation for the group of viewers.

"HELLO! HELLO!" The volume of the Estate Agent's voice startled me. Goodness knows what the neighbours felt.

"Good morning," I replied. "I thought Tarquin was managing the viewing?"

"He was but his wife put her foot down," he chortled. "Something about a 50th birthday celebration in Claridge's.

So, I'm covering for the old man. My name is Owen, and this is Patricia and her daughter Melanie."

"I need to ask you to take your shoes off," Owen said, "we have so many viewings booked that we'll ware the carpet thin if we leave our boots on. Metaphorically speaking of course." Owen laughed at his own joke whilst I looked perplexed and thought. *"This is the only viewing appointment booked today. Where are the other viewers hiding?"*

"Of course," Patricia complied with the request and nudged her daughter to take off her sandals. "Selling your home is stressful, the last thing you need is to try to get stains out of your carpet."

I gulped, and my face reddened. "Thank you. Please come in. I'll leave you in the capable hands of the expert." I pointed to Owen and continued, "one request, please do not touch the blind in the bathroom. I need to replace the fitting."

Owen's sales banter sunk into the background as I fiddled on my laptop, searching for a new blind and requesting various quotes from removal companies.

"Oh, it's a lovely home," Patricia declared. "Don't you think love?" Melanie did not sound as enthusiastic as her dominant mother. "We're looking to get her on to the housing ladder, this will be ideal once Pete has finished with it. We wanted dad to come along today, didn't we love?" Melanie nodded more out of habit rather than agreement. Patricia continued her monologue. "Sorry, I should explain. Pete, my husband, is a builder. Always busy. Wouldn't take him long to get this place modernised. Especially with Uncle Phil and his son – only eighteen but can turn his hand to anything and is such a great laugh, isn't he love?" Melanie stared at the floor and gave the distinct impression she wanted to leave immediately. Owen picked up on the theme of modernisation and put forward suggestions, "you could put a flat screen television on that wall, and a long sofa along here. With new ceiling lights and upright radiators," Owen looked disapprovingly towards the stain on the carpet and continued, "new flooring would really make the living space look brighter and bigger. So much potential. "Melanie could not tolerate the strained atmosphere any longer and went to the door.

"Don't you want to look at the bathroom again, love? We can plan the style of the new bath and shower."

Melanie muttered, "I'm gonna be late."

"Oh yes, of course," her flustered mother replied. "Got an appointment with Susie. They're like gold dust – she's so popular. Do you know her? The one on the High Street?"

"Yes," I replied. "She's a good friend."

"Oh, that's good. How long have you lived here?" she asked. "Ten years." My voice quivered with recognition of the seismic change.

"Where you moving to?" Patricia asked.

"That's a work in progress. Lots to think about." Owen's picked up on my earnest expression and he read my non-verbal message of "please leave now!"

"There'll be no problem with a quick sale, would there Mary? Tarquin says you have the option to stay with family." Owen's arrogant attempt to manage my future plans rattled me and I ushered him out the door.

I slumped in the cosy armchair and sipped the extremely stewed coffee which tasted awful but not as bad as the feeling in the pit of my stomach with regards the dilemma of moving. *"Oh no,"* I thought. *"The next viewing is at midday."*

The oven clock showed 12:30 p.m. but it was prone to going at its own pace so checked my mobile. I telephoned

Owen "Please can you confirm when the next viewing is taking place? Tarquin told me it was at midday."

"No, they've cancelled," he replied. "I mentioned it earlier?"

"I don't think so," I hesitated, "but there was a lot going on and my head is all over the place."

"Tarquin will call you next week to give you an update and positive feedback. He needs the sale to make up for the last few months. No longer the golden boy!" Owen sounded gleeful in sharing the news about Tarquin's misfortune or mismanagement of his sales.

"Oh, right," I mumbled at the unexpected appraisal of Tarquin's missed sales targets. "Don't worry Mary, I'll put him straight at the team meeting on Monday. The boss will want to be kept in the loop."

I was not aware how far down the greasy pole Tarquin had slid. It did not make any sense – The choice of Claridge's for a birthday celebration does not reconcile with low or no commission?

"He didn't take Edie to a coffee shop for her birthday never mind Claridge's," I thought. Tarquin cannot afford another divorce; I suppose a weekend on the credit card or cards is the worst of two bleak scenarios.

Thick brown packing tape twisted around the scissors and entangled in the string holding together a batch of Royalty magazines dating back to 1981. If I pulled the tape too quickly it would rip the print from the fragile front cover which did smell damp: the garage was a great space but did not provide the best storage solution. I had to battle through mould and cobwebs and spiders which were a ridiculous size. The ring from the landline was muffled under the large roll of bubble wrap: I had knocked the handset off the bookshelf during the afternoon. By the time I released myself from the packing tape, string and wrestled with the swathes of bubble wrap the sound stopped. Immediately after the intermission in the noise interrupting part twenty-two of my packing project, my mobile ring tone gradually increased to the point of annoyance.

"MARY, good evening. Owen from Dale Estate Agents. How are you?"

"Who?" I replied rather abruptly.

"Owen Notin. We spoke on Monday. I'm just calling to confirm the viewing at 6:30 p.m."

"I do not have a note of a viewing?" I ruffled through my rucksack to find my diary to doublecheck.

His tone changed instantly. "You must be confused. That's the trouble with using old paper diaries. You probably threw it away with the rubbish from your flat."

I was riled by his patronising tone and said, "the OLD diary may be handwritten but at least it is not a product of A.I. and cannot be hacked into and changed."

"Yeah, whatever," he retorted. "The potential buyers are with me now. We'll be around in about 15 minutes."

"It's not convenient," I snapped. "The floor is filled with packing boxes." I stopped providing an explanation. *I do not have to justify myself to him.* I thought.

"Your call. But you've probably lost a sale." He continued with his sales manipulation – trying to pile on the pressure. "Don't say I didn't warn you."

"That's most kind," I quipped. "I'll take the risk. From now on all appointments need to be confirmed in writing; I mean e-mail. Not sure if your age group could write a letter!" Not surprisingly he slammed the phone down and I popped a sheet of bubble wrap in frustration.

***

"Alright mate," Quenton Seal, the manager of Dale Estate Agents called out from his office.

"No, I'm not!" Owen's voice cracked with anger. "Why on earth did you agree to put that paranoid old woman on our books?"

"Which one?" the manager chortled.

"Miss, I'm not Mrs Danick or whatever her name is?" Owen leaned against the wall; drained from another day without a sale.

"Oh, Mary Danrich," the manager replied. "Bit of a favour for the old boy. He better increase sales soon or head office will be having a word. And I'm not letting him drag us down."

"Never mind dragging us down, he's weighing us down," Owen replied. "Have you seen the

state of that flat? It's a dump!"

"Tarquin will get rid it," the manager said with a slight hesitation over-shadowing his usual overbearing self-confidence.

"Talking about me buddy?" Tarquin's announcement as he walked into the office took Quenton and Owen by surprise. "Nothing bad, I hope? No one on the shop floor – we might miss a sale, lads."

Quenton, the manager, was not amused at Tarquin's wise crack. "Ah, the wanderer returns. Thought you were living the high life in Claridge's. What are you doing here? Missus thrown you out?"

Owen smirked, "don't worry, buddy, I'll keep her company."

Tarquin's false grin strained the muscles around his jawbone and masked his insecurity about his beautiful younger wife. "Very funny. My wife is perfectly content. Just thought I'd pop in to see if I'd missed anything?"

"We do have telephones," the manager looked quizzically at his colleague who did not look as if had enjoyed a relaxing weekend amidst the luxurious setting of Clarridge's.

"Thought I could pop into a few punter's homes, see how they are getting on," said Tarquin.

"You can start at 36 Castle Court. How are you going to get a sale if she's always busy?

"Not convenient!" Owen mocked Mary's voice and continued his diatribe, "pompous oldie. Then going on about writing letters or something stupid like that! Where did you get her from, mate?"

"One of the in-laws. It'll be a quick sale -she'll do what I say. I have told her to move out to make it chain free – attract more attention. But in the meantime, don't be so gullible – don't fall for her lies. It's all an act – just like her sister. Two sides of the same coin. Paint me out to be the villain of the peace whereas they are the Witches of East Wickham!"

"Don't worry about that, mate." Owen replied. "I ain't going anywhere near that flat again. You're on your own with that one and you're welcome to it. Anyway, have to go to meet the couple who wanted to view Castle Court." Owen turned towards the manager and proclaimed his game plan to gain attention, but also to humiliate Tarquin again. "I'll make up an excuse about the cancellation of the viewing and walk along the High Street with them – get them interested in the area and show them the new builds near the station."

"Good man," the manager replied. "That's what we need – thinking outside the box See you two bright and early tomorrow. Team meeting at 8 a.m. Just received new sales targets and we're going to beat them."

***

"What did you say to him?"

"I told him he can't write a letter," I replied sheepishly.

"Talk about winning friends and influencing people. You're not going to get a good deal by insulting the Estate Agent. Come to think of it, you're not going to get any deal with that numpty, Tarquin, selling your flat."

"He might be a numpty, but he can sell an ice-pop to a polar bear." I laughed.

"Not funny. Never mind him and commission, have you had anything to eat this evening?"

"Crispy jacket potato with cheese, "I replied. "The baked beans looked tempting but thought best not."

"No, definitely not," came the curt reply. "No buyer would tolerate that smell. What have you done today, apart from being rude?"

"Fighting with the packing tape. It's really strong, and I lost the battle and tore the page of one of my old Royalty magazines, "I wined.

"No wonder those old things haven't fallen apart after spending years in a carboard box in your garage. Your mum offered to buy the official folders, but old Miss Independent said she'd sort it out!"

"I am too tired to argue about the content of my garage, again. I am a bit stressed and got a lot on my plate. It's a good job you are my best friend otherwise I would have put the phone down." I quipped.

"You're so kind! You can have my plate of stress if you want – you're welcome to take it. Would love to see how long you would juggle all the plates spinning in my life. Right, moan over. I'll come over with Andy on Saturday and we'll get you sorted."

"It's the Wimbledon final on Saturday, Andy will be watching, won't he?" I asked.

"The women's final, it'll most likely be over in thirty minutes. We'll come later in afternoon."

"Don't be so sexist!" I chuckled. "Thanks, it'll be a great help. Andy can manage the operation."

"Don't be so silly. The only thing Andy will be managing is his mobile, if he ever gets the hang of it, to keep any eye on the football results. Right, moany minnie, I've got to go now – to manage a house, not like some, who have teeny weeny flat to clean." Nicola's tone mellowed and her final message was, "take care. Yeah? If you want anything or need to chat. Call me. Anytime. Even if it is to talk about the price of milk."

"Thank you," I whispered.

***

Nicola Church has been my friend since 1980 She worked in the group department of Britus Assurance Company before I moved to that office. We rubbed each other up the wrong way initially especially on the topic of the British Royal Family and general comments about Trade Unions, strikes, the excess of capitalism in the City of London etc. But we shared the same work ethic which was the foundation of our friendship. She was fiercely feisty and most men in the department feared the infamous fiery feedback especially when delivered in the middle of the open plan office. Not tall in stature but a giant in fighting for the underdog in the office especially the younger girls who were taken advantage of in more ways than one. But to give her, her due, she stood up for the men who were intimated by the louder brash characters behind their desks. I think she knew about Mick, I think most people in the company knew about Mick's behaviour. Eric made sure his reputation was revealed.

Nicola did not pass judgement, well not initially but as we spent more time together and banter entered the acceptable boundaries of our friendship, she asked me forcefully, "WHY?"

"Why what?" I retorted.

"Why didn't you stop it!" Nicola barked.

"Wasn't really anything to stop," I sighed. "I don't know really. It was my first week in the office when he first wowed me."

"We are talking about the same Mick Fuller?" she asked with brutal directness. "Please tell me you are not pining over him,"

I hesitated and looked over my shoulder at the other guests in Burger King, in Lower Regent Street, and said slowly and unconvincingly, "uhm, no."

"He's married!" Nicola's raised voice caught the attention of the staff behind the counter.

"Would you like to put a notice on the menu board and then everyone can join in?" I snapped.

"Sorry," Nicola said and lowered her tone. "He's not only married but looks like a reject from a seventies' cop drama and no longer has a career in Britus Assurance Company or any other firm if Eric has anything to do with it."

"Why don't you just say what you think for once," I chortled.

"Mary, there's plenty more men, I mean single men, your age, and you never know they may even respect you. The Christmas party is coming up soon. You might bump into Neil under the mistletoe!" Nicola smiled cheekily.

"Who?" I asked.

"Don't play the innocent with me; Miss, butter wouldn't melt in my mouth, Danrich."

"Oh, yeah. Neil. His friends with Andy, isn't he?" I stared directly at Nicola who was blushing profusely. "You know, Andrew Church? But you haven't given him a second glance, have you?"

"Don't be silly. Of course, I know Andy," Nicola replied sharply. "He takes the payment requests to the banking team. I have to talk to him. I can't send him a message using morse code."

"You'll have to come up with a better excuse than that," I sniggered. "Would be a match made in heaven – your surname is Bishop, and it would change to Church?"

Nicola looked flustered and pulled at the sleeve of her blouse and said, "this silly button, I'll have to get mum to change it again."

"Nice try at changing the topic," I teased.

"The only thing I want to change is this blouse; it's driving me mad!" Nicola replied and reached towards my packet of French fries. "Let me help you finish those – don't want them going to waste do we?"

***

Packed in like sardines was an apt description of the Christmas Eve afternoon drinks in The Trafalgar pub. This was an extreme introduction to team bonding with my colleagues in the Group Department. It sounded such fun but stuck in a crowd of intoxicated office workers was not proving to be enjoyable although I smiled to try to fit in. By the time I arrived there was absolutely no chance of getting drunk because I could not get near the bar.

"What kept you?" my team leader shouted. Nigel had a booming voice but amongst the mix of cheering and singing along to 'Merry Christmas Everybody' by Slade, I could not hear what he said so I just nodded. He laughed and indicated with his hand he'll buy me a drink. I raised my thumb in recognition. I felt so sorry for the bar staff who were trying to collect empty glasses. They were shoved around like the silver metal marbles in a pin ball machine. A young man walked towards me with a tall tower of pint glasses, and I stepped back to give him an inch more room. He seemed to be so relieved. I stumbled and heard a yelp, "OW!"

There was not the space to turn around. I said, "I'm so sorry, whoever you are."

"Think that's put an end to my ballroom dancing this Christmas!"

The voice, what I could hear of it, sounded familiar. I felt a hand guide me back towards a much sort after space by the window The touch was gentle – not a grab; did not feel lecherous. "Sorry," he said. "I thought it best to get you out of the line of fire, so to speak."

"Felt like I was in the battle of Trafalgar for a minute," I laughed, edged sideways and locked eyes with Neil Bach. "Thank goodness, it is someone I know," I said with a sigh of relief. "Didn't fancy getting stuck in a corner with a complete stranger."

Neil's broad smile helped me relax and he said, "not a complete stranger but we have not been introduced properly. I saw you at the Christmas party but did not want to interrupt you and your boyfriend."

"Boyfriend?" Even though Neil could not hear me fully he got the gist of my confused expression.

"You were sitting next to him at the restaurant?" Neil's enquiry made its way through the wall of sound.

"No, that's Simon." I squeaked. "You know Simon? From Policy Payments?"

"Think so," Neil could not join up the dots.

"He promised Eric he'd go," I said, "he's one of Eric's shining stars. He really wants Simon to work in Group but don't think he'll leave Policy Payments. Think he is in line to be a deputy manager next year. Group is a different kettle of fish."

"We don't smell that bad!" Neil laughed and I joined in, as a recognition of his quick wit.

"Simon is very happily engaged and getting married next year. So, no, not my boyfriend." I am not sure if Neil heard part or no part of my explanation, but he smiled politely.

"Can I get you a drink?" he asked.

"Thank you," I said, "but you'll be at the bar until New Year's Eve at this rate. Nigel is trying to get me a drink or hopefully drinks."

"Okay," Neil replied and offered an alternative refreshment, "do you want a sip of lager to keep you going? Sorry, not the nicest way to get to know you, but it might help to cope with the noise."

"Cheers!" I said as I took the untouched pint of lager from the window ledge. The taste was not pleasant, but it balanced up the social interaction i.e. we were both holding pint glasses.

"MARY!" The volume of Nigel's voice had turned up a few notches. It made me jump. "I didn't have you down as a beer drinker?"

"I'm not," I replied. My words were inaudible, but my team leader understood the shake of my head.

"Is he leading you astray?" Nigel elbowed Neil and winked and then passed me two double dry martini and lemonades. "The girls said this is what you have. Alright?"

"Yes, thank you." I raised my thumb again because it was impossible to hear my squeak above the raucous celebrations.

"Come and join us," Nigel shouted. "Neil will never let you go, if he has his way!"

Neil's face and neck reddened, and I felt sorry for him, but I was well aware of the banter amongst the men in the Group Department.

"I'll be there in a little while," I said. Neil ushered Nigel away which I thought was amusing. Nigel could be quite hands on, but his eyes were firmly set on Janette, the incredibly bubbly, blond, and curvaceous, new secretary to Mr Kindon; the Manager of the Group Department.

"Are you okay?" Neil asked.

"Yes, thank you." I sipped my martini and said, "that's better."

"Do you like working in Group?" Neil asked.

I nodded. "Lots to learn."

"Sorry, what's that? Can't hear you in this noise!"

I felt awkward but leaned closer to Neil. "Lots to learn!"

"Not lots to earn, sadly!" We both laughed. "Not on my grade anyway," he said.

I was not sure if he was trying to have a subtle dig because of my recent promotion before I moved to Group but was far too distracted with the overwhelming atmosphere to consider that point any further.

"Where's Nicola?" Neil asked. "You two are usually together."

"So you've been keeping a check on us?" My attempt at a joke sounded completely inappropriate once the words left my mouth. "Sorry," I said quickly. "That sounds terrible. I mean, I thought everyone was too busy in the office to notice what is happening."

"Sorry, my fault," Neil said. "I was glad Nicola helped you and was friendly to you. Some over there can be a bit bitchy, if you get what I mean?"

"Yeah, Nicola warned me," I said. There was a break in the music which lessened the celebration slightly but was such a relief.

"That's better, "Neil sighed. "Do you want a cigarette?"

"Yes please," I replied. "We better be careful, otherwise we'll put burn marks in our clothes."

"Good point," he said. "Could you keep my pint on the ledge for a minute, gonna take off my jumper, hope you don't mind, it's boiling in here!"

"Wey, hey!" Nigel shouted. "Bit early for your strip tease show, Neil!" The team laughed but most importantly Janette giggled and stared at Nigel in admiration. He had got past first post.

"He's horrible to you," I said.

"Don't worry," Neil replied, "there will be pay back, and he knows it! Andy will help me."

"Where is Andy?" I asked.

"Oh he's on the other side of the bar with the darts team."

"There's so space to play darts," I shrilled. "He'll hurt someone!"

"No." Neil laughed and held the cigarette in his mouth at the same time which reminded me of John Travolta in Grease, although he was not Mr. Cool in the Group Department. That title belonged to Nigel, my team leader, but Eric Nadler, the Director, surpassed his rating by a mile. I found it strangely comforting that Neil was not the cool guy, he was Neil – not a slave to an ego but a sensitive soul with an armour of protection and reflection, of course, like most people.

"Andy was looking forward to seeing Nicola. He thought she'd be with you?" Neil said with a hint of melancholy on behalf of his best friend both inside and outside the office.

"Ah, that's shame," I said. "She had to go home to look after her mum who's got flu. Sounds as if she hasn't come to terms with being a widow. Nicola is so caring."

"And so sharp!" Neil quipped. I sensed he was trying to lighten the mood therefore I raised my glass and said, "Cheers! Happy Christmas."

"Can I join in this private Christmas party?" Andy leaned over his friend's shoulder.

"Yes, of course," I said. "Cheers!"

Neil looked at Andy and said, "only if you're buying, mate."

"Don't call you Scrooge for nothing," Andy knocked Neil's arm.

"Don't call me Scrooge at all!" Neil quipped. "Make mine a pint!"

"Right," Andy smirked. "That's half a pint for Mr Bach and what would you like Mary?"

"Dry martini and lemonade, please," I replied. "Sorry, I did not think you knew my name."

"Nicola talks about you a lot, not in a bad way, promise!" Andy laughed.

"Been having many intimate chats with Nicola, lately?" Neil teased

"Only about payment cheques. What are you talking about?" Andy tuned into Neil's line of thought. "Not that again, I've told you before!" At that exact moment, the music resumed with the record, 'Stop The Cavalry' by Jona Lewie. "Right, I'm off," Andy trotted down the step into the mass of customers.

"We'll never see him again," I joked. "I should be so lucky!" Neil followed up the statement. "I'm joking, don't mean that at all. He's a great friend. Just wish he would get the courage to ask Nicola out."

"Don't blame him," I said, "she's a bit scary."

"Bit!?!" Neil exclaimed. "She's terrifying. Even Mr Kindon is scared of her!"

"Oi! That's my friend, don't be nasty. Where's your Christmas spirit?" I nudged Neil in the ribs and quickly withdrew my hand. Although, slightly woozy, I still had enough awareness to be cautious after what happened with Mick. Nicola would have slapped my hand away.

"Hopefully, Andy is getting my spirits at the bar. He knows the Landlord so will be in with a good chance to get served before midnight!"

"What are your plans for Christmas?" I asked

"Usual," Neil replied. "Home tomorrow with mum, dad, and big brother unfortunately. I think his girlfriend is coming over in the evening but don't think my mum and brother can stand each other for that length of time."

"Oh dear," I said. "Sounds a bit awkward. What are you doing Boxing Day?"

"That's more relaxed." Neil's tone lightened. "Dad and me go to the pub lunchtime. A few beers with our neighbours, a few rounds of darts and a few packets of crisps."

"What?" I asked. "After all the food on Christmas Day and you're having crisps?"

"Yeah, can't beat a pack of cheese and onion crisps. You think that's bad; dad has pork scratchings. Really winds mum up!"

"Yuk!" I grimaced. "My favourite is salted peanuts."

"Must remember that" Neil said softly. You would not normally associate salted peanuts with a romantic moment but there was nothing normal about the setting or the person standing in front of me. At the time, I dared not think he was different in case a wife popped out of the woodwork. But he was younger than me therefore could be too young to be married but did not want to make any assumptions.

"And what about you," Neil asked. "What are your exciting plans for Christmas?"

"At home tomorrow with mum, dad, sister, grandma, and grandpa. We usually go to my grandparents because grandma's roast dinners are out of this world. Well, not quite but are very tasty. But mum wants to give them a rest this year." I took a breath. "Sorry, I'm babbling. Basically, a family Christmas."

"No other halves?" Neil enquired eagerly.

"No." I confirmed. "We do not have other halves; that s Edie and me."

Neil's broad smile seemed to widen if that was indeed possible. "Good to hear," he said.

"Oh, is that the time?" I exclaimed, hoping the large clock above the bar was wrong.

"Yep, nearly 3 o'clock," Neil said. "Time goes fast when you're having fun."

"Sure does. Sorry, I have to go; promised to help mum. She's not going to be happy."

"No problem." Neil replied. "My mum would prefer me to stay out until the evening, she says dad and me get under her feet. Which station are you going to?"

"Charing Cross," I replied. "Hope the trains are still running."

"I can go to the station with you, if you want?" Neil put forward the suggestion tentatively. "We can find some form of transport together."

"Do you mind?" I asked with a mixture of surprise and happiness."

"Don't mind at all," he smiled.

"Mate, where you going?" Andy shouted over the heads of the other customers. "Got your drinks here!"

Neil mouthed, "I'll call you," accompanied by the miming of holding a telephone handset. Andy initially shook his fist jokingly and then winked at his friend with a slight touch of envy that his friend had plucked up the courage to be with the girl he had fancied from the first time he saw her walk into the office.

"Thank goodness," I shrilled louder than anticipated. "There's a train at half three. Thank you so much for coming to the station. Really nice talking and shouting with you."

"Yes, great to have a chance to meet you properly, even though I couldn't hear half of what you said," Neil quipped.

I tapped his arm. "Cheeky. Have a lovely Christmas." I instinctively kissed him on the cheek. My natural blusher glowed brighter than Rudolph's nose.

"And you. Have a great Christmas. When are you back in the office?" Neil asked with an eager anticipation expression.

"Supposed to be 5th but told Nicola I'll cover for her next week if she needs to stay with her mum." I replied in an official manner which I regretted because it sounded as if I was trying to book a business meeting.

"Okay," Neil replied with a patience that surpassed his youth. "Maybe we can go for a drink over a packet of peanuts, salted ones of course!"

"Yes," I responded with glee. "I look forward to it."

Neil leaned over to kiss me on the cheek, but I turned my head quickly to look at the platform information board. His lips brushed over mine for a fleeting moment and he whispered, "sorry."

"No need to be sorry," I said softly. That was a nice Christmas present.

***

The Christmas of 1980 was quite surreal. Lovely being with mum and dad. As usual, grandma and grandpa spoilt us with too many gifts. Mum tutted her disapproval and dad laughed quietly so not to upset mum too much. Grandma noticed how distracted Edie and me were.

"You're not really here are you, girls?" she probed into the reason for our different moods.

"Sorry, mum. What was that?" I asked.

"Mary, I am your grandmother not your mum. Are you feeling okay? Do you need to lie down?"

"She's done enough laying down!" Edie's caustic remark prompted grandpa to defend me.

"Edie. There's no need for that! It's Christmas day. This is precious family time – do not waste it. Mark my words, young lady, it will fly past before you know it."

We were all taken aback by the stern reaction from grandpa but respected his maturity and wisdom

"I have looked at the evidence in front of me," Dad said jovially. "I put it to the jury that they are in love!"

"Dad!" Edie and me protested at the same time with our faces burning as hot and bright as lava.

"I rest my case," dad laughed and tapped his spoon on the dinner table in place of a gavel.

Edie was intrigued why I was so keen to return to the office and I was even more interested in finding out why she was making phone calls late at night in the living room with the door closed. Mum and dad refused our requests to have telephone lines installed in our bedrooms. She also asked me to go to the sales in Bromley with her which was completely out of character. I refused because I enjoyed being with grandma and grandpa – his words seem to have a sense of urgency, and I sensed he was trying to share news with us.

***

I did return to the office on 29th December. To my delight so did Neil. No matter how much I tried, I could not stop thinking about him and it was not in a crude physical desire either which made it all the more confusing. He was not the stereotypical adonis and I was no beauty queen, but the connection was considered and caring. It took us both by surprise, especially at such a young age. He was sixteen and I was seventeen, shouldn't we just be having fun, going out with groups of friends, and dating their friends. We went for lunch a few times a week and he would buy small bags of salted peanuts and discreetly place them on my desk as he walked past. I beamed and he nodded in recognition. Nicola was over the moon and kept asking when we were going to go out for an evening or meet during a weekend. I kept asking her when she was going to meet Andy for a drink. "He hasn't asked me!" she complained regularly. "Well ask him!" I retorted. "You're bold. Maybe too bold – you'll scare the poor bloke." No matter how many match-making manoeuvres Neil and me tried, the two of them stubbornly refused to budge. "I give up!" Neil said to Andy.

There was an offer of overtime on Valentine's Day. I suppose a distraction for all singletons who felt sorry for themselves. Neil, Andy, Nicola, and me put our names forward.

"What is the matter with you?" Nicola asked me. "Why isn't Neil treating you to a meal or a day out?"

"We need the money first, before we arrange a fancy day out," I responded. "So, we thought, we'll go to The Trafalgar after work for a game of darts. Do you want to come with us?"

"Darts?" Nicola shrieked. "Who plays darts on Valentine's Day?"

"We do!" I retorted. "Andy will be there."

"Gets even better," Nicola moaned in frustration. "When people ask, where did your boyfriend take you on your first date? I am going say, to play darts! Brilliant!"

"Wait a minute," I said, "who mentioned '*a date*' and who mentioned '*boyfriend*'? It's just a group of friends going out after work."

"Whatever!" Nicola stormed off.

"We're making progress," I thought. "She'll crack soon."

Nicola refused to send Andy a Valentine's card, but Neil finally persuaded Andy to leave a chocolate heart card on her desk before she arrived in the office. The fact that I bought the chocolate heart card was neither here nor there, Neil had finally got his friend to make a move. I thought, "*they must seriously like each other if it is taking this much trouble to encourage them to get together and make their feelings public.*"

***

The slam of the neighbour's front door made me jolt up from the cosy armchair. I had nodded off at an awkward angle and my neck stiffened. "I must get the clothes ready for the charity shop, Jo will through a tantrum if I'm not ready when she is at the door." My tendency to speak to myself or air my views to the empty auditorium has increased considerably since dad died. The neighbours are used to my eccentricity and think they are quite keen not to have to deal with my '*off-centre*' characteristics for much longer. As I tell people, "I am off centre but do not mean any harm." I now say it before they think it. Pointless trying to hide my different approach to social interaction which raises to the surface now and then. More frequently during the last year. *"Maybe best I do pack up and leave the country?"* I thought.

The tightly folded clothes in the black storage bags on top of the wardrobe were part of my *'iconic collection'* i.e. the ones I could not bring myself to give away. The first out of the bag was my grey pin stripe suit; faded but in fairly good condition.

"I can't," I thought and then reality kicked in when I looked into the mirror and said out loud, "if you got run over by a bus tomorrow, do you seriously think, Jo is going to stand here and sort out your clothes? Get real! She'll put them in sacks and give them to the Restore & Recycle company." I reluctantly filled up the large sports bag for the charity shop. I did not want to arrive with lots of plastic carrier bags filled to the brim. Jackets with distorted shoulder pads, and short shorts – the days when my legs could compliment summer holiday clothes, and tee-shirts with faded prints of overseas resort names, were moved in readiness to leave. The bridesmaid dresses from Edie and Tarquin's wedding and Nicola and Andy's wedding were non-negotiable. At the bottom of the storage bag was a black dress wrapped in tissue paper. Sections of the diamante decorative pattern on the front had fallen away but as I held the dress against my body, the memories of my 18th birthday party were not far away.

***

Nicola and me had planned to take an afternoon off to go clothes shopping for my 18th birthday party but she had used up all of her accumulated flex-time credit and holiday allocation for the month to take care of her mum. But she made sure to give me fashion tips or instructions.

"Remember, subtly sexy. Not too short, not mid-calf. Definitely not low cut, and best to cover up some of your arms. And if you buy one of those 'Bucks Fizz' skirts I'll disown you!"

"Promise?" I said cheekily. "I don't care what you say, I'm buying black tights with a diamante seam!"

"Be my guest," Nicola replied knowingly. "The speed at which you go through tights they'll only last five minutes. No one will have the chance to notice them."

***

Dad booked the ballroom at the Bromley Court Hotel. He insisted. I wanted to reserve an area in The Trafalgar pub, but dad did not want grandma and grandpa travelling to the centre of London to stand in a packed pub under a cloud of cigarette smoke. "We could go to your favourite country pub for a family lunch on the Sunday?" I pleaded.

"Do you think there may be a risk of you and Edie slouched over the table with a hangover?" Dad cross questioned me with such finesse it was irritating beyond belief.

"No!" I reacted far too quickly and jumped straight into the trap set out before me. Dad peered over the top of his glasses and said calmy, "would you like a moment to reflect on your reply?"

My face crumpled with frustration and recognition – he was right as always. "Dad," I said. "I love you, but you are so annoying!" I hugged him and he said, "surely not all the time?"

"No, not all the time but most of the time." I giggled and thought I'd strike whilst the iron was hot. "Dad, can we have a DJ?"

"Yes, of course. But it is on condition there is subtle background music whilst grandma and grandpa are there." Dad sounded as he was reading out terms of a legal document.

"Okay," I groaned and muttered, "gives me more time to chat to Nicola."

"Iain, the hotel manager has arranged for a specially trained cocktail waiter, so you can treat your friends to those fancy drinks with umbrellas and sparkles." Dad offered a morsel of compensation and then asked out of the blue, "will your young man be joining us?"

"Neil?" I mumbled and paused before thinking of an appropriate reply. "Yes. I can introduce him to you and mum. I've asked him to bring his friend, Andy, for back up."

"We're not that bad!" Dad laughed. "Please give grandma some information about him in advance. I do not want her interrogating the poor boy; I apologise, man. I have invited great aunt Josie and her husband Bertrand. They should keep grandma occupied."

"NO! Dad," I shrieked. "Please, not Aunty Josie. She'll ruin it by criticising my clothes and hair and weight and anything else she can think of on the night. And then tell Neil he needs to find someone his own age who is thinner! What have I done to deserve this?"

"Remember what I told you?" Dad said, "control your emotions. Each time you go into the flustered state, those surrounding you, waiting for the moment to pounce, will step in, and take the floor, and steal the show and your reputation."

"Yeah, I know. But she doesn't go after you," I groaned.

"Why do you think that is?" he asked and waited with keen anticipation, in hope his coaching had sunk into my mind.

"Because you're a man and you know Bertrand's boss?" I mocked with a confused expression.

"That may be the case, but the main reason is that she does not get a reaction."

I looked down, disheartened – I had a fluctuating temperament that I could not always keep locked in the self-protection box.

"You'll be fine," dad offered a hand of reassurance. "Whatever you do, please let mum know which drinks Neil and his friend, Andy, prefer and the type of food they like? Oh, I forgot to mention, mum has booked a few bedrooms in the Bromley Court Hotel. We do not want guests struggling on the trains especially during the bank holiday weekend. Please let her know how many rooms you need for your friends. The budget cannot stretch to the entire hotel."

"I know, I know!" I replied. "That'll be great. Nicola can have a sleepover here. Neil and Andy can share a room. Don't tell Aunty Josie. Goodness knows what stories she'll be making up!"

***

My 18th birthday was a contained celebration. I felt Neil and me were being scrutinised; not by all guests but the atmosphere was somewhat strained at the beginning of the evening. My relatives and family friends made the most of catching up in an environment where they could hear each other. The buffet was nice. The star prize was for grandma's cakes. The manager kindly allowed mum to bring a small selection of home-made food. His decision was motivated by the fact that mum selected the top price buffet per head and pre-ordered numerous bottles of champagne and wine. The section of the bar dedicated to cocktails, attracted

Nicola and me. Not only because of the handsome bar man, but the broader variety of drinks and decorations in the colourful glasses, brightened the atmosphere. I could hear Aunty Josie tutting from the other side of the room. Andy teased us, "he'll drop one of those bottles in a minute; then you won't be giggling. Especially if your dad has to pay for the breakages." Nicola turned her back on Andy and retorted, "Why are you such a grumpy old man? Go on and get your lager and leave us alone. We're having fun."

"I'm not old!" The twenty-one-year-old Andy protested.

"Okay, I'll give you that, "Nicola grumbled but the rest is true.

After Andy shuffled over to Neil to get his pint of lager, I said, "Bit harsh?"

"Firm but fair," Nicola replied.

"Fair?" I asked. "Give him a chance, he's only trying to break the ice."

"Don't be silly," Nicola quipped. "We're work mates. He talks to me in the office."

"About work," I mumbled in frustration, and then turned up the volume, "I give up!"

"Ladies, pretty ladies," the cocktail bar man cheerily called us closer. "No time to quabble. It's time to party. What can I get you?"

"The word's squabble," Nicola corrected him in her headmistress tone.

"Ssshh," I interjected and pushed Nicola's arm off the bar.

Neil wore his navy suit with thin white pin stripes, a white shirt and thin navy-blue tie. It really did not bother me that was his office attire and appreciated the effort to be presentable to meet my parents. Andy wore a black suite, white dress shirt and black bow tie. Nicola was not impressed, and I was slightly worried Andy was making a bit too much effort. However, grandma and Aunty Josie were delighted at his fashion sense and hesitated before referring to Neil's lounge suit. "These modern factory-made suits are so versatile, but can get threadbare quite easily," Aunty Josie exclaimed as she looked at the elbows of Neil's suit.

Grandma was quite reserved with regards the questions she asked Neil. I think mum had given her a pre-party protocol guide with the added footnote that it was a fun celebration for my 18th birthday. There would be plenty more opportunities, hopefully, to ask questions. Grandpa and dad were respectively polite to Neil, as expected. The topic of sport is always a good distraction and can achieve a certain level of connectivity although Neil's support of Queen's Park Rangers football club did not sit too comfortable with them, they enquired about points and players and match fixtures. Mum was far too busy moving from guest to guest to ensure everything was alright. "Where's Edie?" Mum's increasing level of stress was palpable. "She promised she would be here before the guests arrived!"

"Probably putting on another layer of make-up!" I said with glee.

Nicola stepped on my toe and then offered to help mum which she gratefully accepted. I nudged Andy and gestured him to go with them, thinking a shared experience helps to build a relationship. "Don't know what to do!" His reluctant reply prompted Neil's response, "give me strength! Help carry a chair, carry a glass, carry a serviette – anything!" Andy shuffled off in pursuit of Nicola.

"I wonder if he'll stop her coming?" I whispered to Neil.

"Sorry, who?" asked Neil.

"Tarquin," I replied. "She's changed so much since December."

"Will be sad if your sister can not be at your party," said Neil. "And I could've met them."

"Here's your chance," I stuttered as I saw Tarquin and Edie at the door. He wore a black tailored tuxedo with satin silk-faced peak lapels, white cotton evening shirt with pleats on each side with two-button '*cocktail cuffs*' (turnback cuffs) and black silk butterfly-shaped bow tie. The highly polished plain-toe slip-on shoes with raised heels and high vamps decorated with a self-strap across the instep, reflected the last rays of sun light shimmering through the patio doors.

"He'll have a "*vodka martini, shaken not stirred*" Neil said in his best Sean Connery accent.

I laughed at his amusing comment and complimented his impression. But I was distracted and worried about Edie's outfit. "That's not Edie," I said.

"Sorry?" said Neil. "Your mum is being extremely affectionate with a guest whose name is coincidentally Edie?"

"Oh. No, I mean. It's Edie, but she looks so different!" I spluttered out my confused mixture of thoughts.

"I think you may need a double vodka martini," Neil said softly to soften the angst on my face. He put his arm around my waist slowly, conscious some guests were watching his every move.

Edie's long sleeved, high necked and ankle length dress looked like a remnant from a convent. The only difference was the colour – the pale blue made Edie look even more anaemic than she had been since February.

Aunty Josie was over the moon with Tarquin's choice of dress code and lapped up the fantasy tales of Tarquin working towards owning a multi-million property empire. "My time is my investment for the future. No time to waste. Every minute is money." He rattled off one cliché after another.

"Please can someone shut him up!" I groaned.

"I'll shut him!" Nicola ranted.

"NO!" I replied sharply and a bit louder than intended. I coughed to cover my tracks. "Please, leave him alone. He wants the attention, and Edie will be on the receiving end of the fall out later."

"The DJ should be starting soon," Andy said awkwardly.

"Oh, Andy, trust you," Nicola chortled but with distinctively softer edges surrounding her rebuke.

The tinkering on the side of a champagne glass with a spoon prompted us to raise our heads. My initial thought was, *"oh, no, they're going to sing Happy Birthday!"* but then I changed to a more optimistic vision, *"grandma has made one of her fantastic fruit cakes and it will have incredible icing and decorative flowers…"* My hopes were shattered by the sound of Tarquin's voice. "Ladies and gentlemen, if I could have your attention, please." He annoyingly tapped the champagne glass again – louder and longer. "Ladies and gentlemen, please, I would like to make a very important announcement. Me and Edie are beyond excited to announce our engagement! Isn't that fantastic news?" There was a ripple of applause. I walked up to dad and whispered, "please, dad, stop him. He's not even asked Edie!"

Dad purposefully positioned himself beside Tarquin and strategically shook his hand and took the microphone away from him. "Well, thank you Tarquin. I would like to take this opportunity to thank my wonderful wife for all the superb arrangements for this enjoyable evening. All her hard work is much appreciated and needed. You know what they say, behind each successful man is an even stronger woman." The guests laughed before dad continued. "We are here to celebrate my youngest daughter's 18th birthday, goodness where has the time gone. The minutes merge into hours and then days and years. They gather and migrate to another sphere leaving us holding precious memories which no one can take from us, even those embarrassing moments and photos we would rather not look at again." He leant down to pick up a briefcase and I nodded my head. My ashen face mouthed the words, "Please no! Please!" Dad smiled and said, "I'll save those for another day! On behalf of your grandparents and your mum, it is my pleasure to raise a toast to my darling daughter, Mary. Wishing you the happiest of birthdays."

The guests raised their glasses and in unison cheered and said, "Happy Birthday!"

Dad coughed, "Oh, before I forget; you may be eighteen, but we still expect you home at 11 p.m. You know your older sister, Edie, will provide us with evidence! On that note, ladies and gentlemen, I thank each and every one of you for making the effort to be here. Battling through the engineering works on the trains and road works is no mean feat – hats off to you. For those staying in the hotel, Rosalind, my wife, has organised complimentary drinks and supper to be delivered to your room, please ring reception when you are ready. Have I forgotten anything, darling?" Mum nodded and smiled. Dad continued, "enjoy the rest of your evening. And, Mary, the first dance is booked with your old dad, yes?"

I blushed profusely and nodded.

"Is that my que to leave?" grandma directed her question at her only child, "you know, subtlety is not your strongest attribute."

"Margaret. Leave the poor boy alone," grandpa touched his wife's arm gently. "He is walking on a tightrope of family politics with a few new pieces on the chess board."

"Darling, that, is the most confusing mixture of metaphors, even for you," grandma replied. "Okay, I am going. In fact, I am looking forward to sitting down on a comfortable chair with a cup of hot tea. We do have a chair in our room?"

"Yes, of course, mum," dad affirmed. "Rosalind has booked you a suite. Only the best for you."

"Flattery, especially false flattery is not one of your strongest attributes either."

"Grandma, thank you so much for coming," I stepped in to save dad. "Lovely to see you in your elegant evening dress."

"You are most welcome, darling," grandma replied. "I hope your young man has complimented you on your magnificent diamante decorated dress?"

"Yes, grandma," I said. "Neil said I look nice."

"Just nice," granddad intervened, "you look beautiful. He needs to fine tune his etiquette."

"Oh, Gilbert, don't be silly," said grandma in a huff. "He's just a boy!"

"Okay grandma," I sighed. "I will see you tomorrow for one of mum's great Sunday roasts but nowhere near as fantastic as your cooking. Please don't tell her I said that."

Grandma and grandpa laughed. I hugged them and kissed them on the cheek. Nicola rushed over to the DJ and gave him the green light to get the party started.

Dad and me stepped around the floor, a scaled back version of a waltz, to the song 'What a Wonderful World' by Louis Armstrong. Mum had tears in her eyes and think Nicola took so many photos she used a roll of film. Halfway through the song, I whispered to dad, "please ask Edie to dance, I think she needs you right now." Dad obliged and the relief on Edie's face was telling.

Tarquin smirked and called out, "Steady, Edie. Don't want you falling over in your condition!"

"What did he say?" I said with a startled look on my face.

Nicola could no longer contain her anger. She turned to me and said, "your mum was asking for you. A couple of guests are leaving and want to give you, their presents. She's by the reception desk." Neil went with me; he showed a mature understanding far beyond his years.

Nicola tugged at Tarquin's arm. "Watch the cloth!" he said dismissively.

"Watch my mouth!" Nicola retorted. "I don't know what your game is. No, wait a minute, I know exactly what game you're playing, and you've just lost. You know where the door is. Bye!"

"Who do you think you are?" Tarquin snapped.

"Well, I'm the woman who saw you on the train last week with the blond girl" Nicola frowned when Tarquin laughed in her face and said, "you've had too many cocktails, darlin.' You'd better go and have a lay down!"

"Oh, I've a better idea. Why don't we go and tell Edie's dad about the girl. Maybe we can all meet up for a drink one day, that'll be nice, won't it?"

"Don't be so stupid! I'm an Estate Agent. We meet lots of clients, and now and then I go the extra mile. It's called customer service."

Nicola's face filled with a red rage, "I tell you exactly what you are. You are a liar and it's not customer service you're interested in; it's commission. Oh, by the way, do schoolgirls buy property?"

"You're mad," Tarquin snarled.

"Oi, mate," Andy interjected much to Nicola's surprise. "That's enough. I am calling you a taxi and you're getting into it. You ain't ruining this evening. And before you start, I was on the train with Nicola. My uncle's a teacher in Bromley and we can easily trace the school badge. So, it's your call!"

Nicola looked stunned. Andy winked at her and walked closely behind Tarquin to the reception desk.

"Where's he going?" I asked. Nicola was speechless which was a new experience. "Nicola, are you okay? Earth calling planet Nicola, are you with us?"

"Sorry. Yes, sorry," Nicola stuttered and took a deep breath.

"Where's Andy?" asked Neil. "You haven't frightened him off already?"

"No," Nicola replied and walked towards the reception area without any explanation.

"Do you think she is alright?" I asked. "I should go after her?"

Neil rubbed my arm gently and said, "don't worry, they'll be fine."

Dad sat by the bar and was engrossed in a conversation with work colleagues and friends from the rugby club. Mum chatted with Susie Beatty, our family hairdresser, and Miss Drake from Drying Days & Sewing Streams.

Miss Drake re-tailored my black dress to reduce the split in the skirt and toned down the glaring diamante design, so I did not look like a glowing beacon.

Nicola and me danced enthusiastically to songs ranging from 'Stand and Deliver' by Adam Ant, 'Don't Stop the Music' by Yarbrough & Peoples, 'Ain't No Stoppin' Us Now' by McFadden and Whitehead and of course, 'Making Your Mind Up' by Bucks Fizz.

I asked the DJ to dedicate the song, "It's a Love Thing" by The Whispers, to Nicola. She was not amused but still danced enthusiastically.

A few work colleagues dropped in for about an hour: they were on their way to an opening of a night club in Croydon. Mum was extremely happy when Nigel and the bubbly Janette left. She gave me a disapproving look after looking at the diminished content of the buffet. I shrugged my shoulders.

Dad tapped me on the shoulder, "I am going to see if Edie is okay. Will you be alright?"

"Where is she?" I asked with a slight irritation that dad's attention had shifted to her again. But the concern for Edie far outweighed the selfish and envious thoughts.

"She mentioned going to grandma's room," dad replied. "I'll go and check. Are you enjoying your party?"

"Yes, thank you so much, dad," I slurred slightly. "Sorry, too much champagne."

"I have not seen your young man dance. Not a Fred Astaire then?" Dad laughed.

"His name is Neil," I muttered. "And you know that. He's warming up his dancing shoes. Give him a chance."

"I know," dad said tenderly. "Give your mum and me a chance to get used to him, and accept our baby is in a relationship. I doubt if your grandparents will ever get used to it!"

I smiled and rested my head on my dad's shoulder.

"I heard that," Nicola sniggered.

"What exactly did you hear, big ears?" I teased my friend who was slightly unsteady on her feet after too many cocktails.

"Your daddy, called you baby?" Nicola giggled.

"Right," I said firmly. "I'm getting you a cup of coffee. No, wait a minute, I am going to ask Andy to get you a coffee."

"Okay, thank you," Nicola replied.

"What?" I asked. "You're not going to have a tantrum?"

"Ssshh!" she whispered. "It'll be nice. But he betta' bring back a cake or he'll be toast!"

I giggled, "you are so funny, and catty, at times, in fact, most of the time, but I love you!"

Nicola staggered against my arm, "I'm not the only one you love, am I?"

"What are you talking about?" I asked impatiently. "And for goodness' sake, take those sandals off, you'll end up in hospital with a sprained ankle. Everyone's seen the sparkly heels so you can take them off now."

"Don't avoid my question," Nicola sat down with a thump into the back of the chair. "Ouch! Oh yeah! What was my question? Ah, that's it: Neil. You love him?"

"We haven't discussed that topic yet?" I replied sheepishly.

"TOPIC!" Nicola squealed. "It's not a project meeting!"

"Please keep your voice down," I said. "We are taking things slowly. And it's lovely. So please do not spoil it."

"Tonight, is an ideal chance to discuss the topic?" Nicola's catty remark made me bring out my claws.

"Don't be so ridiculous," I snapped. "My grandparents are staying in this hotel, and mum's friends will have their radars out. Where is Andy supposed to sleep, in the garden?"

"You're such a defeatist," Nicola complained. "You have to think outside the box."

"What box is that?" asked Andy. "Are we having a work meeting?"

I looked at Neil and said, "Would you like to dance?"

"Not really," he replied but think it's better than sitting at this table.

The DJ was onto the retro part of the evening so the first dance with Neil was, "Summer Holiday" by Cliff Richard which was released in 1963. "Specially for you, Mary!" the DJ called out loudly. "1963 – a vintage year!" A surreal moment that I will not forget. Neil saw the funny side of the situation and did an impression of Cliff Richard which eradicated some of the embarrassment. I gestured to Nicola to join us. She pushed her sandals under the table and pulled Andy up off his seat. The next song was 'Vienna' by Ultravox, which is a great piece of music, but it orchestrated an awkward moment when the words, *this means nothing to me. Oh, Vienna,*" reverberated around the floor. I shook my head towards the DJ and thankfully he turned off the record before the upbeat part of the song started. Our quartet of the sidestep dance could only cope with a slower rhythm.

"Ladies and gentlemen," the DJ announced. "You have been a great audience. Sadly, we have to play the last song of the night. Come and join the birthday girl for one last waltz."

Neil stood in front of me. We hesitated. The song, "Too Young" by Nat King Cole wrapped around our emotions. Nicola grinned; she pleaded guilty for the choice of music. I looked at dad and he tipped his head forward respectfully, as if to say, "it's your time."

Neil placed his hand on the small of my back and held my right hand. My cheek rested against the side of his face and purred, "mmm"

"We're not too young, are we?" he asked sensitively. The intonation of innocence etched into my heart.

"No," I replied. I squeezed his hand and closed my eyes.

***

CHAPTER 6

Droplets of rain tapped on the opened balcony door. I could not get to the gap before the downfall drenched the edge of the carpet. The tangled beaded chain on the blind caught the side of my slipper, and I fell against the small coffee table

"Boop! That's not supposed to happen." I thought.

The clock on the oven showed 10:22 a.m. I picked up the sponge by the sink and cut a small piece of the Scotch Magic Tape. The sponge was more effective dealing with the rain-soaked carpet, than the tape in repairing the torn strip of MDF on the table leg. There was eight "more minutes before open day was scheduled to start. Tarquin had booked numerous viewings today. "Bit awkward?" I said to him. "Not awkward," he quipped. "A winner!" he declared loudly as he ended our mid-week sales catch up, on the telephone, which I dreaded more and more.

"MARY!" MARY!" There was absolutely no need for an intercom when Tarquin shouted my name outside the main entrance to the flats. I pressed the door release button and could hear him galloping up the stairs.

"HELLO! HELLO!" Tarquin shouted with the same velocity even though he was standing next to me. I waved my hands towards the floor in hope the gesture would encourage the volume to be turned down. A foolish wish. Tarquin continued with his instructions. He resembled a tour guide telling the lost tourists where to go. "Shoes off, guys!" Tarquin looked at the six potential buyers and the pile of shoes caused an obstruction in the shared hall. I pointed to the corner by the water meter cupboard and the group complied with my silent request.

"RIGHT! Let's get this show on the road!" Tarquin called out as he walked past me. "We'll just walk around – that's okay, isn't it?" A statement of intention not a respectful question. I nodded my head and grabbed my rucksack from the living room. It is doubtful if Tarquin carried out any type of character background check – that would have taken up his time and we are reminded at every opportunity how every minute is his money.

"Please!" My squeaky tone caught the attention of the man pulling at the heavy blind in the bathroom. "Please do not touch the blind. I can move it to one side if you want to see the window. Or if you stand by the hall window you can get a better view of the window frame."

"Well, we normally inspect all the window frames!" the middle-aged pristine gentleman continued with his objection. "It's mould, you know, that black mould, porous, contagious, unsightly and the smell – it's dreadful."

I stared at him and thought, *"anything else?"*

"Mary, leave this to me," Tarquin said and ushered the gentleman wearing a burnt orange blazer into the hall

"Nice flat. How long have you lived here?" asked the elderly gentleman in a more genuinely interested tone.

I returned to the living room and replied, "ten years in December. It's gone so quickly!"

Two women were on the balcony, and I gave out a health and safety warning, "please be careful, I have been cleaning the floor this morning." This was true but I was also hoping to distract them from the loose telephone wiring hanging down from the roof: one of the many jobs on the 'to do' list for the management company.

"Oh, hello again," I said. "I didn't see you in the crowd, sorry, I mean group at the door."

The mother, Patricia Parrot, and daughter, who had viewed the flat on the previous Saturday smiled. "Yes, there's a lot today. Melanie wanted to bring her dad, didn't you darling?"

"Nice to meet you dad," I said, "always good to get a professional opinion."

His daughter walked towards the kitchen.

"Please excuse her manners or lack of manners," the mother said in an apologetic tone. "It's all the stress. Told her she can stay at home as long as she likes, but she wants to live on her own. Melanie, where are you darling? Let me come and inspect the kitchen with you."

The father smiled, and I acknowledged his long-standing patience with the characteristics of his wife. "You don't mind if we take photos?" he asked. "I think Tarquin said there are more people arriving soon; we won't be able to move. I can take my time to look at the dimensions and potential for to make a few tweaks here an' there. You know what these youngsters are like, large flat screen tv on the wall, internet in each room, everything grey, even the carpet!" We laughed and I wondered if he was having a subtle dig at the ever-deepening green patch on my fading cream carpet.

"Please, go ahead," I said, "but don't take photos of the safe containing all my jewels."

"Are the white goods staying?" the couple called out in unison from the kitchen?

"Uhm..." I hesitated. "Maybe. Need to think about everything."

"But you are selling the property, aren't you?" came the disgruntled enquiry from the husband rattling his car keys in his hand. The wife appeared to be more agitated and confronted Tarquin. "This property is for sale and not just for review?"

"Yes, of course, absolutely, 110%," Tarquin's over exaggerated catch phrases hid his anger about my hesitation. "We'll secure the best deal. No problem! And that includes the white goods. Mary can't wait to buy a new fridge to go into her new home"

The intensity of the rattling of the keys lessened and the husband asked, "have you got a moving date?"

"No!" I replied sharply and speedily before Tarquin had the chance to make up even more fairy stories. "It's a work in progress."

"Won't be a long wait," Tarquin interjected, "I've already got properties lined up for Mary. I'll keep in touch each week, and you can call me, anytime. You've got my mobile number."

I shook my head slowly, exhausted by the lies. The gentleman with the burnt orange blazer had left. My intervention in the bathroom ruffled his feathers and the vintage style bedroom dismayed him. Tarquin ticked off the list as the viewers whittled down to the mother, father, and long-suffering daughter. "What do you think?" I asked the daughter directly. Instead of her mother answering for her, a strained voice rose up from the hall, "you don't have to answer that question? You can provide the feedback to me directly when we get back to the office."

Her father was perturbed that the Estate Agent was directing his daughter's speech and movements. "We're going straight home," Peter Parrot replied sternly.

"Of course, of course," Tarquin's apologetic, almost grovelling, tone clung to the air like an unpleasant smell. "There's lots of new properties on the books. I want to give you the descriptions leaflets – hot off the press! I don't want you to miss out."

"Oh, don't worry," came the reply. "I do not miss out on anything for my children." He nodded and smiled at me. His wife and daughter scuttled after him.

The rattling keys echoed in the hall. The couple did not say goodbye to either me or Tarquin. "How many more?" I asked wearily.

"Loads!" Tarquin reeled in delight. "Could you make me a coffee? I have to answer these calls."

I handed the mug of strong black coffee with three sugars to Tarquin as he sat at an awkward angle, in my soft cosy chair. "You're a star!" he winked at me as he replied.

Raised blood pressure thudded through my head, and I clenched my eyes shut.

"Hello, excuse me." A timid voice emanated from the hall. The young man looked anxious. "Is there anyone there?"

"Oh, hello," I replied. "I assume you're here for the viewing?"

"Yes. Think I am too early? There is a large group outside the main door but the man with the white hair said I could leave my bicycle inside, under the stairs, for a few minutes. I had one stolen last month and can't afford to go through that experience again."

"Welcome," I said. "Have a quick look around while you've got the space."

"Thank you so much, Owen in the office said I can come along." The relieved cyclist rushed around the rooms. Tarquin looked confused and when I explained it was a referral by Owen, he looked annoyed.

"I'll bring the other's up now," Tarquin's advance warning filled me with dread

"HELLO! HELLO!" It did not matter how many times I heard Tarquin's spiel it still grated. "Shoes off, guys. We've lots of viewings today. The old carpet cannot withstand the heavy footfall."

This group consisted of eight people. I stood guard at the bathroom door. Even though there was a note on the window blind asking for it not be moved, curiosity got the better of some viewers.

"Where are the best schools?" a couple asked.

"Sorry, I don't know," I replied with a cautionary sub note. "There are no other children in the block. It's not really a child friendly property."

"Oh, it's a very friendly location," Tarquin intervened and listed off the names of schools showing in the result of his search of the internet.

A mature lady looked lost in her thoughts as she stared out over the balcony,

"If there are any questions, please ask." I said quietly.

She sighed, "I could put a few pots out here and bring a few of the garden gnomes to make it feel more homely."

"Did you have a big garden?" I asked.

"I still have the garden, dear," she murmured. "It is our retreat, Cedric spent hours working on the beds and the blooms on the roses are the best I have ever seen, He worked so hard last Autumn giving them a good hair cut!"

"There are roses in the shared garden," I said awkwardly. "The neighbours would be delighted if someone could help look after them."

"I'm afraid he will not be looking after any more roses, my dear," she said, "well, not in this domain. He passed away in February."

"I am so sorry. The grief is all so raw. How long were you married if you don't mind me asking?"

"Sixty years. We hardly ever argued. Well, Cedric said I argued, and he listened," the widow smiled softly. "We loved each other right up until the end."

"It must be incredibly difficult leaving your home?" I said earnestly. "Is there any way you can stay there? Sorry. It's none of my business. Please excuse me but it is incredibly sad to listen to, goodness knows what it is like to live through."

"My dear, I would love nothing more than to stay in our home. I don't want to move but my son said it's time to move on. The large house is a family home – not suitable for one person. He went into Dale Estate Agents, and they have been arranging viewings for our home. My son said they have potential buyers bidding against each other already – we'll make a large profit."

I wiped away the tear rolling down my cheek and coughed. "I am so sorry." I could not help but repeat my feeling of sadness at the selfishness of her son and the lack of consideration by the Estate Agent. "Sorry, I just need to say, the lift does not always work and the noise from the Garage Services company can get quite overbearing at times. I do not want to stop you finding a new place to live but this is not the most comfortable place to live."

"What are you saying now, Mary?" Tarquin burst into the room. "Please, Mrs, uhm, Mrs uhm. Can you remind me of your name again?"

"Mrs Whiles," the widow whispered.

"Ah yes! That's it. I'm afraid my secretary has your name on my list as Mrs White. Honestly, what am I going to do with her? Anyway, Mrs Whiles, Mary is overthinking things and is worrying too much. The management company have promised they will install a new lift before the end of the year."

"Really?" I asked.

"Yes, or course," Tarquin replied. "I don't know, Mrs Whiles, you would think Mary doesn't want to sell the property

"At least I would still be an area, I have known all my life," Mrs Whiles said. "My son has been talking about me living in Eastbourne. Lovely for a holiday but I do not want to leave East Wickham."

"I understand. There are so many changes to deal with, so would be nice if one thing could remain familiar." My line of enquiry had a purpose. "The High Street has changed a lot but there are a few traditional shops left. Do you know Drying Days & Sewing Streams?

"Goodness me, my dear, yes. I cannot remember the High Street without Miss Drake. She has been so kind. She has come around to our home to mend the curtains. My son said we had to make the place look smarter."

"I entirely agree," I said. "Miss Drake is a generous soul and has an incredible gift. I am so glad she can help you."

I miss dad each day, but at moments like these I miss him even more. He would know what to do, who to contact and what to say or more importantly not to say until receiving legal representation. I made a mental note to contact my nephew, Sebastian. He must know someone who can protect Mrs Whiles.

"Are you two still chatting?" Tarquin asked.

"Yes," Mrs Whiles replied. "We were saying how kind Miss Drake is. I assume you and your colleagues go to her to get your suits professionally cleaned?"

"Used to," Tarquin said loudly. "She used to take my trousers down!" Tarquin roared at his own joke and the three students viewing the property joined in the hilarity.

"Lads, lads," Tarquin chortled. "Before you get the wrong idea and put it on my socials, she's the dry cleaner. She mends clothes."

"Nice one mate!" one of the students said as he gave Tarquin the thumbs up.

The depths of Tarquin's insensitivity knew no limits.

"You finished lads?" Tarquin asked. "Makes a nice bachelor pad, doesn't it?" There was a muted response, but Tarquin persisted. "Are you lads off to the pub to watch the Wimbledon final?"

"No, not for us. We like something a bit faster and more fun," the spokesman for the students replied.

"Well, lads, I've got tickets for Wimbledon tomorrow – the men's single finals. I'll be in the Royal Box – you'll see me on TV. Will be great fun during the afternoon – mixing with the A-listers and royalty."

"Right. Okay." The spokesman did not sound impressed and edged towards the door.

Tarquin's mobile interrupted his boasting. "Cheers mate," he said. "What's the matter with him? Ain't, he heard of Google Maps? Anyway, it doesn't matter, got plenty of coffee and biscuits here. If you get any more punters in, send them over, we'll squeeze in as many as we can."

"Okay, I'll go downstairs to get the next batch," said Tarquin. "That should be it for today. But we've got one straggler who can't read a map apparently!"

"HELLO! HELLO!" Tarquin's booming proclamation reverberated around the entrance hall.

The notification ping on my mobile showed the text from Nicola, "How's it going?" Followed by a mixture of emoji hearts and a cheeky face.

My response message, "HELP! Please make it stop!" Nicola replied, "I'll call later" with more emoji hearts.

Another four viewers pulled at the hall cupboard doors, kitchen cupboards and blinds in the living room. One lady insisted she keep on her walking boots and was more interested in the condition of the ceiling and flaking paint in the hall.

"Absolutely no need to worry," Tarquin speeled off what the viewers wanted to hear, "The management company are going to carry out all the repairs before the end of this year."

Some of the viewers looked as if they were visiting a museum, some were professional viewers – it was almost a full-time occupation, and some were genuinely searching for a new home – fresh start.

"I've booked a company to clean the oven this week," I said after a couple wafted away the smell of salmon from the baking tray, "I know the owner," Tarquin chipped in, "top bloke. You won't recognise the old thing! It'll look brand new."

"I'll get that," Tarquin said. I did not hear anything. Tarquin continued, "I'll buzz you in – top floor! Best to use the stairs."

Two sisters looked around the bedroom and asked, "are you leaving the wardrobes?"

"I'm not sure," I replied. "This one is on its last legs. Bit weighed down with old clothes – my decluttering project is not going that well at the moment. One of the charity shops organises collections – I'll have to give them a call."

"She needs that for her old make up bags!" One sister nudged the other one and giggled. It was nice to have a moment of light relief.

"Come on ladies," said Tarquin, "time to go. If you're interested, I've got plenty more to show you!"

The sisters giggled loudly. My face straightened and I looked at them, and said, "please do not encourage him, and please be careful of him!"

"She's only joking ladies," Tarquin squirmed. "Aren't you Mary? She's got such a dry sense of humour. Anyway, we're wrapping up here, unless you want to stay and show this young man around. He's a bit late to the party but you never know he may seal the deal today?"

"That is kind, but I prefer to look around on my own, if that's okay?" The voice sounded familiar, but from the distant past, not a recent recollection.

I turned and blinked twice. No words came out of my open mouth.

The warmth of his blue eyes fixed on my dazed expression.

The giggly sisters held onto each other as they put their ridiculously high sandals on. They called out, "Thank you so much! Good luck with everything!" I walked to the door and said, "Thank you. Take care and hope you find somewhere to live soon." I stayed by the door, shook the mat and eavesdropped the conversation between Tarquin and the last potential buyer of the day.

"You did not give me advance notice of an open day?"

Tarquin replied impatiently, "I apologise if you misunderstood the directions. Did you seriously think it would just be only you'? We're in 2023 – the property market is completely different compared to the 1970s."

"I will bow to your experience" came the reply. "I was not able to get my foot on the first rung of the bunk bed ladder in 1970, never mind the property ladder!"

Tarquin pouted like a spoilt child. He liked to think he had the monopoly on sarcastic comments. "Right, it'll have to be a quick look. I have a viewing at the next property in ten minutes. You can always come back another time – is that okay Mary?"

"Yes," I mumbled. "Tarquin will make the appointment."

"Thank you," the gentleman sounded grateful, and his smile broadened.

"Right, let's make sure I've got your mobile number," said Tarquin. "I just need to check your surname. My secretary's written down Book?"

"Nearly. It's Bach."

"Cheers Neil," Tarquin replied. "I'll give you a call."

***

"Well, how did it all go?" Nicola's enthusiasm was not refreshing my fatigue.

"Don't ask?" I moaned. "Please don't ask!"

"Stop being silly," Nicola said, "I ain't called you to talk about the weather!"

"Well, beside, them nearly pulling down the blind in the bathroom, slipping over on the balcony, wrenching open the door of the hall cupboard, and complaining about the smell of the oven, it all went well."

"By the sound of it, you got off lightly," Nicola quipped. "And your oven does smell. You can't deny that!"

"Guilty as charged!" I replied. "It'll be cleaned this week."

"Anyone really interested?" Nicola asked, "not there for a nose around someone's home."

"Don't know really. He had too many people here. I think it put people off – don't know how it's supposed to help." I moaned and put my feet up on one of the dining room chairs.

"How was Mr super salesman?" Nicola laughed.

"Annoying," I replied. "No, I take that back; he was excruciatingly annoying." "Go to another Estate Agents!" Nicola demanded attention but was sharing her concern about my wellbeing in her own indomitable style.

"I know! But sometimes the salesman you know is better than the salesman you don't know. At least he is charging less commission, and love him or loathe him, he will get a good price for the flat even if it is a bit tired! He knows so many people in the area – he's more likely to get a buyer by word of mouth – not the internet."

"You can always re-decorate, might get a few extra pennies for your piggy bank?" Nicola voiced her suggestion again. She had tried to encourage me to at least paint the door frames or buy new kitchen cupboard doors, after dad passed away. Anything to brighten up the flat.

"Really don't think it's worth it," I said. "One girl brought her parents. Her dad said she would re-decorate the entire place – she wants it to be all grey, flat screen tv, Alexis – you know all that stuff."

"Alexis!" Nicola chortled. "It's Alexa. You're such an old granny at times!"

"Stop tormenting me," I groaned. "I've had a yuk day! And who are you calling a granny? It's your 60th birthday soon and I want an invitation to your party!"

"What party?" Nicola exclaimed.

"You know, your party. It'll be the talk of the town," I said and then pleaded, "please have a party, pretty please. I need something to look forward to and a chance to dress up; put on my best diamanté dress which I found at the back of the wardrobe!"

"If you're talking about the dress you wore at your 18th birthday – you're in fantasy land. Firstly, how are you going to fit into it? And secondly, why have you still got that old thing? You're meant to be decluttering?"

"I am clearing out loads of clothes. It just so happens my 18th birthday dress is in the iconic category in my wardrobe."

"No!" Nicola replied. "No! I am not taking the bait. I need to cook Andy's dinner."

"I'm sure Andy wants you to have a party. September is not that far away – he'll need to start getting things sorted."

"Mary, how long have you known Andy?"

"Too long," I replied.

"Exactly!" said Nicola. "And at what stage did Andy organise a party? An afternoon tea? Or even a cup of tea? I love him dearly but think you are talking about another Andy. I'll chat to the kids, think they'll like the idea,"

"Andy can show off his best 'dad dancing'." I said, "and can be a bit of a reunion for his mates."

"I'll ask him to do a bit of match making for you," Nicola chortled.

"Don't you dare!" I exclaimed. "I am up to my limit with what I can cope with. Finding Mr Right is not even on the list of things to do. That ship has sailed a long time ago!"

Nicola and me continued chatting about the chaotic scenes from earlier in the day and what I could and what I should do about the flat. It didn't take long before my eye lids weighed down with exhaustion, and Nicola abruptly ordered me to go to bed when she heard me snoring.

***

Nicola Church (nee Bishop) married Andy on Saturday 24 June 1989.

After a tentative start their relationship blossomed. They are different in height, temperament, and interests, but a mutual respect and deep understanding has formed a strong bond. Andy is a gentle giant but is fiercely protective when it comes to Nicola.

A simple but suitable wedding in Swanley. Nicola asked me to be a bridesmaid, but I could not tolerate the teasing of my family, *"always the bridesmaid and never the bride."* Mum and dad, Edie and her seven-year-old son, Sebastian, were guests. Tarquin was too busy. "Saturday is super sales day!" he declared when he saw the invitation.

I had not foreseen Nicola as a typical June bride, but Andy selected the date because it was his best friend's birthday. Neil and his wife were guests of honour and Andy enjoyed leading the chorus of 'Happy Birthday.' Nicola's facial expression tightened, she held my hand and said, "You okay, mate?" I could not speak but rested my head on her shoulder.

"She'll seek damages for the cleaning of the dress," said dad in his attempt to alleviate the pain.

"Could you recommend a good lawyer?" Nicola quipped.

"Of course!" Dad said precisely and professionally. "Only the best for you!"

"My darling daughter," dad took my hand, "it is time I presented my serious dad dancing."

I smiled in recognition of his loving tactic for a distraction, "a waltz will be just fine, dad."

***

My relationship with Neil Bach crumbled in 1986. Maybe we were too young for the relationship that we needed or just too different? My rebellious streak can disintegrate into self-destructive behaviour which is almost too much for others to tolerate unless they have an unusual supply of empathy or willingness to listen. The problems Neil had with his mother and brother caused tension and I did not know how to handle it effectively at that stage of my life. The fractious life of Edie drained a lot of energy from my family. I spent a lot of time babysitting for Sebastian, who was born in November 1981. Whilst Edie was traumatised by the ex-marital affairs enjoyed by Tarquin, Neil was shoved to the side, in some ways, to ensure Edie was safe or protected. After our relationship ended, dad contacted Neil to apologise for the pressure put on my shoulders to 'save the day' and invited him to reconsider after a pause. Neil declined. I was not grateful at the time, in fact I was devastated, but Neil called an end to our relationship after our holiday to Greece during the summer of 1986. One final attempt to salvage our fading relationship. We had a couple of good nights and even when the DJ in the hotel played the song, 'Only You' by Yazoo – the cherished memories of when Neil gave me the single as a birthday present on my 19th birthday, could not hold us together. The frayed edges were too weak to repair.

Closing our joint account and returning personal items was not only painful but humiliating. I regret not just signing the building society account over to him and let him keep the total amount: our savings for the deposit for our home. Stubbornness and dare I say, pig headiness, took hold and incited some ugly behaviour which I regret enormously. Edie egged me on, but I cannot blame her for my every word and action. Edie was envious of my happiness and Neil's loyal dedication to me. Nicola took a more reserved approach. I think she was more angry at Andy for not doing more to keep us together. Neil listened to his friend for a while but could not cope any more. During the four and half years together, we grew incredibly close and shared idyllic moments which I still hold dear to my heart, and they are as clear as if they happened yesterday. The irony – they were the most modest experiences in unglamorous settings.

In January 1982, a mixture of snowstorms and industrial action resulted in disrupted train services. There were no trains from Kent on some days so Britus Assurance Company organised coaches for a skeleton staff so the claim payments could continue. I battled through the queues and overcrowded buses in the mornings. Edie said I was looking for attention – trying to play the hero. I ignored her taunts and escaped the endless conversations about her two-month-old son. Neil booked a place on the coaches running from Dartford and somehow managed to get me a seat on the evening trips even though I did not have a reservation. Andy gave up his place and squashed on the back seat with his mates from the darts team. Not at all comfortable but there was plenty of hilarity coming from the back of the coach. Nicola got special leave during the disruption due to her mother's declining health. We did our best to cover for absence. Even Andy learnt how to process claim payments which he swore he would never do.

I used to count down the minutes until we left to get the coach. I packed up my bag with cans of soft fizzy drinks and small bags of salted peanuts. We rushed to the pick-up point and always the coach had already arrived so I could sneak on without too many people kicking up a stink. I used to sit by the window and sink into the seat. The large maroon hand knitted scarf grandma gave me for Christmas, made a good blanket. Neil, still in his navy-blue work suit with thin white pin stripes, added a blue, loose knitted jumper and a checked scarf to adapt it to a winter outfit. He used to take off his single-breasted jacket, with a button missing, before sitting down to try to keep it in shape. I used to lean against his chest and curled by legs up by the window. I did not care if the journey took three hours, and he felt the same. We were content. We did not say much – we did not need to. Bizarrely, amidst the traffic jams and icy roads we were calm – it was our time. There were a few comments from colleagues, "Ahh, so sweet – look at the love birds!" Neil ushered them away and knew he had the backing of Andy if anyone really caused trouble, so we were as snug as a bug in a rug. The radio rattled out tunes, most which I cannot remember and at the time did not pay too much attention to. But there was one, "It Must Be Love" by Madness. It became a significant theme song. Andy called it our anthem but only when out of the reach of Nicola. His ribs must have been bruised when Andy was in his 'wind-up' mood.

The patient driver, who was as resilient as a schoolteacher, stopped at a few extra places to give people a chance to get home before midnight. The additional stop near Hither Green station was a great help for me. A few got off at the same time, so it covered my part as stowaway. The driver knew exactly what was going on and Andy said he would buy him a pint: after the disruption had finished. The non-negotiable rule set by the driver was that there could be no standing on the coach. Andy rushed down the aisle when I started to get off and used to say, "kept the seat warm for me?" Neil kissed me before I left my seat and there were cheers of "whoa! Romeo!" But it did not stop him. Neil was not showing affection to show off, he did not need to, we had plenty of opportunity for privacy if organised carefully in advance. He was comfortable showing his affection for me and so was I. It was not crude or over the top. Truly difficult to explain and to replicate. I am not reflecting through rose tinted glasses because I have tried to feel that level emotion again and it quite simply has not happened no matter how much I have tried.

***

CHAPTER 7

"Aunty! Aunty?" Jo's voice knocked the sleep out of my eyes.

"Yes, I can hear you," I replied. "Are you okay?"

"Great!" Jo replied. "Brilliant performance last night! Cosimo was ecstatic so we went to a club after to celebrate. Fantastic night."

Jo was in a hyper mood which is as difficult to deal with as her down days. I wondered if she needed money and dipped my toe in the water, "That is good news. Nice to hear you could let your hair down for a few hours. Those clubs are expensive, aren't they?"

"Yes, they are Aunty. And no Aunty, I'm not asking for money!" Jo quipped.

"You're so cynical," I said. "And you're so right. I worry about you. My budget is restricted at the moment. Moving is an expensive hobby."

"No need to worry," Jo said in an even more worryingly buoyant tone which usually indicated a new love interest or a one-night fling. "Georgios paid for all the drinks, and we were in a VIP booth."

"Sounds like a fun evening," I hesitated. "Dare I ask?"

"Aunty, don't try and act all angelic! Mum told me about all your boyfriends." Jo teased me and knew exactly which buttons to push.

"That must have been a very quick conversation," I replied defensively. "Do I need to buy a hat?"

"Will you stop it!" Jo snapped. "I'll forgive you this time because you're stressed about moving! And to stop you going on' Georgios is taking over as the new Director in

August. He says I should have a more senior role in the production. So, I should be earning big money next year. Oh yes. And he's gorgeous."

"Ah, I see. Gorgeous Georgios!" I chuckled.

"You are so predictable!" Jo groaned. "Why do I bother telling you anything?"

"Did Chen go to the club?" I asked foolishly.

"Next question!" Jo's sharp reply continued, "and I'm asking the question. What is that racket you've got on? If it's the Bay City Rollers, I'm putting the phone down!"

"I'll have you know – the Bay City Rollers did not release anything that sounded like a 'racket'," I said. "It's Madness."

"Who?" Jo asked. "The stress is really getting to you, isn't it?"

"You know," I continued, "Suggs? The band Madness?"

"Of course, 'House of Fun'?" Jo replied. "1980s classic. Some of the *oldies* in the theatre play their songs."

"These predictable comments are catching!" My observation prompted the expected response.

"Ha! Ha! Oh dear, my sides are bursting!" Jo replied. "Anyway, when are you moving?"

"Moving? "I said with a startled squeak. "I'm only on the viewing stage."

"Yeah, I know," Jo replied, "but he'll get your flat sold in no time."

"If you mean your dad?" I chided my niece, "he's working on it. There was an open day yesterday, but it was a mess."

"What? Like your flat?" Jo laughed.

"It might be a mess, but it's, my mess," I said with a sense of sadness. "I'm not sure I want to move."

"You can't stagnate there, Aunty!" Jo exclaimed.

"Stagnate? Makes me sound like a rotten apple," I said. "There's a lot to think about. Need a bit more time to think about it."

"Aunty! How much more time? One year, two, 10 years?" Even Jo's irritation did not sound as scathing as usual. "And how are you going to pay for all the improvements?"

"Might wait until next year. Put the flat back on the market then. It's best to slow down with all this change." I said with a hint of melancholy mixed with fatigue.

"If you get a sale, go for it, Aunty! Don't waste all your money on that flat. Use it to make a fresh start. Live a little."

"Sounds ideal in fairy tale land," I said. "But where I am going to live in the meantime? Might be a bit of a squash on your sofa bed?"

Jo laughed and said, "You can't move in with me. There's not enough room for you and definitely not enough space for your junk!"

"Just so rude!" I said in recognition of my niece's astute observation. "Suppose I could set up camp in the park? No one will notice!"

"Honestly!" Jo groaned. "You can live with Sebastian; he's already offered you a room. Before you deny it, he told me. We do talk sometimes. And if he's too busy I send Seonaid a WhatsApp – she tells me all the gossip!"

"Don't forget you promised to take your niece out for her birthday?" I prompted Jo to consider her family amidst her work colleagues – a lesson learned from my past.

"Yeah, I know. How old is she?"

"Thirteen?" I replied. "Can you remember being a teenager?"

"Cheek! It's not that long ago! I'll sort something out!"

"It's next week." I requested earnestly. "Please don't make false promises, and don't keep her hanging on for months."

"Alright. Okay," Jo replied with a put down, "some of us are busy. I could get her tickets for the Edinburgh Fringe Festival?"

"She can't go there on her own. Her mum is going on an extra teacher training course during August, so she'll be too busy. And before you ask, I am not going!" I put my foot down because I thought it would be nice if Jo could spend more time with her niece.

"I don't want you to go," said Jo. "I want to go to see Aldo. He'll get us tickets. I know she thinks the theatre is silly – I blame Sebastian for that blinkered approach. But she likes the comedy shows; so, could get her into something."

"She likes sport, especially cricket. Sebastian says she is on the cricket team and gives the boys a run for their money. She's won trophies and medals."

"He would say that!" Jo sniped enviously. "She's a daddy's girl."

"Put that jolly green giant back in its bottle," I teased my niece. "She inherited her love of cricket from dad, sorry, I mean your granddad. He would be beaming with pride if he could see her now. Can't you take her to a professional cricket game?"

"No way!" Jo exclaimed. "I'll fall asleep with boredom. It'll be fine – I'll get her to go somewhere interesting!"

"She'll get her own way," I warned. "You've met your match with Seonaid!"

Jo replied, "she'll have to go to a tiebreaker, and I've got more stamina." "Not quite!" I said, "you're just more stubborn!"

"Anyway, Aunty, I've got to go now and get ready. We're going to Sarastro, in Drury Lane, for lunch.

I picked up on the clue, "we," but was not sure how far I should push this. Edie says I should ask more probing questions. It is easy to say but not always easy to do. We do not want to antagonise Jo too much because we instinctively know we'll lose all contact with her, and it'll force her into even more precarious situations than she is in now.

"That's quite a long walk from your flat," I said. "They won't have any place to put your bicycle, will they?"

"No. I'm just around the corner," Jo said hesitantly. Only too aware she was conveying the headlines in relation to a new relationship or liaison."

I heard the background noise from Jo's location – an older man's voice called out, "I'm back darling. Got the croissants and cappuccinos. I'll call Nicos to make sure we get a balcony table!"

"I hope he's remembered the roses," I joked.

"Certainly has," Jo confirmed with joy delivered in every syllable. "Long stem red and white roses!" I heard her whisper, "Thank you sweetheart!"

I mouthed, *"sweetheart?"* And said, "okay, I'll let you go, have a nice lunch and hopefully an afternoon off?" I could hear the man's voice in the background ask, "is that your aunt on the phone? Ask her to join us for lunch?" Jo shrieked, "NO! Sorry. No, she's moving home soon – got loads to do."

"I can't wait to meet him," I teased my niece who was becoming increasingly fraught at the thought of me being introduced to Georgios.

"Bye Aunty, Love you!" Jo took on the role of a loving dutiful niece with an Oscar winning performance. "If you need any help, please call me, anytime. I am sure you'll find a new home soon. It'll be a great move for you. Take care!"

Although not entirely surprised by Jo's new acquaintance, I do worry about her erratic nature. Her mood swings may seem amusing, at times, and I do tease her which does not always help, but it would be nice if one part of her life was settled.

***

The tumultuous years before, during and after the divorce of Edie and Tarquin tarnished their daughter's ability to evaluate relationships rationally and most sadly with little or no self-respect. We all hoped it was a rebellious protest, a temporary blip or momentary attention seeking. Each broken dream and broken promise re-opened wounds. As time goes on, the wounds are becoming more difficult to sew together. The dissolving stitches are no longer strong enough, so the healing process is even more challenging.

Edie was blessed to have support when Tarquin walked out of the family home in 1993. Mum and dad, grandma and granddad reached out and offered to help whenever practical. Dad worked long hours because he became the breadwinner for Edie and her two children due to the lack of financial support from Tarquin. Dad asked a lawyer specialising in family law to send a letter to Tarquin, but Edie did not want to pursue the matter through the courts. She used to say, "best not distract him too much from his work. He's no good to anyone if he is made bankrupt!"

After the paperwork for their divorce was finalised Tarquin married his, already pregnant, second wife. In the space of three years, his new family consisted of a daughter, son and a wife who did not have paid employment. His financial woes were fast becoming unsustainable.

Edie had support and was fortunate not to have Tarquin's relatives breathing down her neck, demanding their rights for access: because they have no interest in his life. But at the end of the day, she was labelled a single mum, treated like a single mum, and was criticised for being a single mum. The branding is not pretty – it deters future male suitors. The treatment is not pleasant – excluded from social events and conversations. She was pushed out of the "mums and chums," group. The criticism is not fair. The gossip mongers did not turn down the volume of their critique and strategically timed their best lines for when they had the largest audience e.g. "If she had looked after him, been more of a wife than a whinger he would not have had to look elsewhere!" The judgement by the officialdom in the Council offices, banks and employment agencies hit her hard. The repeated attempts to justify herself and circumstances sapped her energy both physically and psychologically.

1993 brought a lot of change. Tarquin moved out of his family home, and I moved in with my boyfriend who I had known for four years – a relationship with my work colleague in the company located in the City of London.

I started working for Munich Re in 1987. I had to get away from the Britus Assurance Company near Trafalgar Square. Neil Bach and me were civil to each other but the awkwardness was painful in itself, never mind the emotional torment. When the opportunity opened, I accepted the new role. Lots to learn but the company were willing to train me and the potential for networking was exceptional in a well-established global corporate company. Hence meeting,

Kieran Cael, an I.T. Consultant, whilst I was on a career path to be a Business Analyst and Project Manager. The characteristics in connection with his Asperger's syndrome caused problems, especially in the early days, but we learnt together how to respect boundaries and adapted to a different type of life. Mum and dad were worried, but Kieran's intellectual ability helped him connect with dad.

I felt guilty setting up a new home when Edie's home was shattering around her. I took care of Jo as much as possible, but Kieran was not impressed. "I do not want to adopt a child.," he said, "in fact, I do not want children, full stop!" I empathised with his frustration although he could not empathise or understand why I would want children. At the age of thirty, I was broody. Edie had two children albeit without a husband, my friend Nicola had a son and there was another baby 'waiting in the wings.' Some of my work colleagues were performing the most baffling juggling act i.e. mother, wife, and full-time office job.

My relationship with Kieran reached his limit in 1999. Not really a surprise but when your life turns upside down it hurts, however the washing still needs to be done – daily chores continue no matter how much you want to scream, "Stop! Please give me a break!"

I moved in with Edie. Kieran restored order in his flat with a minimalist décor.

Edie appreciated my help with Jo who was proving to be a handful. Grandma was extremely happy to let Sebastian stay but Jo was another level. But of course, she would help if necessary. Dad did not want to put additional strain on grandma who never recovered after the loss of her devoted husband in 1992. Grandma held on another nine years which was mainly driven by her determination to help with her two great grandchildren. The bedrock of our family was shaken after grandpa and grandma left us.

Edie tried her utmost, but the stress crushed her mental health. After the concern about Jo leaving school at 16 there was a stress of another kind: a celebration in the family to mark another milestone. Usually a pleasant experience, although with all-consuming anxiety about arrangements. Sebastian's wedding to Sophia Frances McKinley took place in 2006. An enjoyable event but it was infected with Tarquin's selfish behaviour. "We can't not invite him!?!" Edie protested. Jo was making the most noise however she was just saying what everyone else was thinking. Thankfully, Sebastian's wife is comfortable in her own skin and takes most things in her stride. No drama – no distractions from her commitment to their marriage which is a joy to witness and a contrast to the sphere of stress encompassing our lives.

I teased my sister when she became a grandmother in 2008. Ewan Hugh Crowmere-Gale was a bonny baby and content. Edie enjoyed babysitting but her weakened frame hindered the amount of time she could carry this well-rounded baby. It uplifted Edie's spirit, temporarily. Mum thrived on being a great-grandmother, but I was not enamoured on becoming a great aunty. I felt like the character in the Oscar Wilde's play, '*Importance of Being Earnest*.' Dad teased me by saying I looked like the character, Lady Bracknell. Jo cottoned onto this taunting and loved to impersonate the famous line, "*A HANDBAG*!?!" It became really irritating, but admit she sounded just like the actress, Edith Evans. A frivolity which led to a few moments of light relief.

***

The dark clouds gathered to disrupt Edie's quality of life and her lack of interest in looking after herself. By 2010, mum and dad could no longer stand by and witness Edie fading away. She had lost her spark and ability to engage fully in conversations. Edie reluctantly accepted their suggestion and financial backing to go to Italy, to convalesce. Dad worked with a barrister who owned a villa in Tuscany. An idyllic setting. The healing qualities of nature are beyond comparison. Edie put off her departure until her second grandchild was born. Sebastian and Sophia introduced us to their baby daughter in 2010. We were delighted to meet Seonaid Rosalind: a feisty character with a loud cry which made the announcement that she did not need much sleep. Sebastian said, "mum, please make the most of the opportunity. With respect, Seonaid does not know who you are – so will not miss you. All we'll be doing for the next six months is feeding, changing nappies, and trying to turn down her volume. And Sophia's mum is coming to stay so we are fully resourced."

Edie heeded the advice from her son and gratefully accepted the gift from mum and dad. A time to recuperate and underpin her life after the subsidence of a toxic relationship with her ex-husband.

***

Signora Concetta Catino, the well-rounded housekeeper, insisted Edie's mobile be kept in the safe. Mum and dad had an emergency contact number and vice-versa. A character full of life and love of nature. She could not understand the addiction to the *Rat Race*. "Who wins?" she would ask and answer, "they are too busy fighting each other to see the finishing line!" She was a wonderful cook but not as good as grandma. Although even grandma would struggle to cook a lasagne which melted in the mouth- smelling of herbs and tasting as fresh as the air. Edie thanked and praised Signora Catino with repeated bursts of, "Bellissima!" Edie's language skills have improved although her accent is much to be desired.

Using her own savings, Edie could not resist a trip to Lake Como and an overnight stay in Villa D'Este. Signora Catino loaned her elegant outfits which were kept in pristine condition after the passing of her younger sister over five years ago. Edie appreciated the gesture but was apprehensive. "I may drop some food on them, what will happen then?"

"We clean and restore them," Signora Catino replied. "They are exquisite hand sewn garments that should be on a stage for all to admire, not hidden in a wardrobe. And, signorina, the management of Villa D'Este will not permit you wearing casual daywear."

"Elegant, and euphoric, enchanting and expensive." Edie's descriptive words included in a good old fashioned post card she sent me to try to convey the sublime and surreal setting of her luxurious stay overlooking the magnificent Lake Como. Edie knows I love receiving letters and cards. E-mails are efficient and snail-mail results in an extended delivery date, but the receipt of post is special – shows someone has made an effort to buy a card, a stamp which can be a trial especially when Edie was in Italy. Although the reception staff in Villa D'Este were pleased to provide stamps and arrange for the postal service. On other occasions Signora Catino took the post for her but insisted the focus should be on her recovery not office work! Edie's mobile was released from the safe on a few occasions so Edie could take photos and post them on Facebook – no doubt hoping Tarquin would see them. It took quite a while for her to block Tarquin from her social media accounts. Clinging on to algorithms was a poor consolation for the destruction and dismantling of her life. Sebastian confided in his granddad – worried his mum was spending time tracking Tarquin's new life which was adding stress to the paper-thin plate she was standing on. Mum and dad were not taken in by the "anti-social" media as they called it. "Lovely to share photos," mum used to say. "We managed perfectly well before. Nothing wrong with photo albums. You can get smaller ones that fit in your bag. I do not want photos seen by strangers." Dad had to engage in electronic communication for his work. He was a whizz using e-mails thanks to Sebastian and could search for information on the internet. Dad's P.A. (Personal Assistant) who also had the role of an Executive Assistant in chambers was a 'superwoman.'

Signora Catino received the parcel cushioned with numerous layers of bubble wrap and brown paper. Inside the box was more bubble wrap protecting a camera. Dad's gift to Edie gave her the facility to capture her adventure on film without curtailing the opportunity to break free. Sebastian tried to explain to his granddad and nan how memory sticks can be used however the transfer of knowledge was not successful. They trusted Sebastian implicitly however were less sure if Edie would keep the 'stickers,' as they called them, in a secure place.

**

Jo kept pestering her nan to pay for her flight tickets so she could stay with her mum, At the age of twenty-two, Jo was sharing a flat with her friends, in Brixton. She had the freedom to enjoy the bright lights of London and reassurance of an open door at her grandparents' home if needed. Edie did not want to sell her family home, so arranged for it to be rented for one year, to keep a safety net in place.

When Jo's strategy to obtain a travel grant from her nan failed, she turned in my direction. She delivered every line in the guilt trip script to convince me to go along with her idea. Unusually, I stood my ground because I normally give into her.

Edie's resilience was broken. The condition could have been described as a '*broken heart;*' however, Edie had sacrificed so much of her talent, her dreams, in fact herself to stand in the shadow of Tarquin Sebastian Jonathan Rowland Crowmere – Gale.

We tried to warn her, but it was like watching rain drops slide off a clear plastic umbrella. The thick waterproof material dulled the clanging of the alarm bells, but we could see the doubt in her eyes; and she could see the fear in our eyes.

I surrendered! The pressure from my niece was intolerable. The compromise: we arranged to meet her mum in Florence. I booked a hotel in the centre as a treat and my niece busied herself by building a schedule to ensure she did not miss out on the famous sites. Jo has a genuine love of the arts but her longing for likes on her social media accounts comes a close second. There was no way we were going to get her to put her mobile out of line of sight and I would not trust any hotel room safe. A vastly different residency compared to Signora Catino who was increasingly becoming an honorary member of our family.

The first item on the itinerary – to visit the Ponte Vecchio Bridge. Ticked box and took photo. Second item – Piazza della Signora. Ticked box and took photo. I cannot get the scene from Hannibal out of my mind. Dreadful to darken the delights of a fabulous setting with a gruesome image. The haunting melody of Vide Cor Meum – music composed by Hans Zimmer stays with me, but I will not push the musical masterpiece from my memory. I was exhausted and overheated by the time Edie arrived at our hotel. My niece was excited to see her mum. I should have booked them a twin room due to the amount of time Jo spent in her mum's room. I naively thought Jo would want privacy, just in case she met, 'Signor Giusto' The One! I did not want to endorse her to have casual liaisons but was not blinkered – was not in denial of her boyfriends she had in London.

Jo booked a table at La Terrazza Brunelleschi, on the fifth floor of the historic Grand Hotel Alighieri. The panoramic windows offer a 360-degree wonderful view over the wonderment of Florence. Jo's interest included the outdoor terrace cocktail bar.

Signora Catino loaned Edie a stunning cocktail dress. She was beaming, her shoulders straightened – freed from the weight of the stress. My white blouse and black skirt did not quite hit the mark, and I could see the disapproval on my niece's face with the invisible sign: "*told you to bring the pastel blue dress.*"

"I feel like a waitress," I said.

"You look like a waitress!" Edie replied with glee.

I smiled broadly – Edie's sassy spirit had returned. Jo interrupted my happy moment with her customary put down. "They don't employ old waitresses – not good for business!"

"Thank you for the insight into employment practices in Italy." I retorted. "Then surely, I must be too old to pay the bill?! Leave it to you, youngsters!"

My niece laughed then looked worried and then sighed with relief when I gave the same smile she had received since childhood.

"Phew!" Edie said. "Close shave there, Jo. You nearly had to use your credit card which I assume is near the maximum limit again?"

My niece deflected the line of questioning and turned the spotlight on me. "Aunty needs a close shave!"

"You are so sweet," I said mockingly. "If I don't pay your bill, washing up duties should settle what you owe!"

"You wouldn't do that to your favourite niece?" Jo asked jokingly with just a slice of angst.

"You are my only niece," I replied. "Well, apart from, Seonaid, my cute great niece who is probably causing a lot less trouble than you at the moment."

Edie interjected, "and no, I wouldn't want to send you to do the washing up because I doubt if you could remember what to do!"

"I am so glad to be here with the two grumpy sisters!" Jo pouted petulantly and resorted to looking at her mobile despite the agreement – *'no mobiles at mealtimes.'*

We ordered tiramisu and home-made ice-cream and, finally persuaded my niece to put her mobile in her handbag.

The band played subtle background music which changed gradually to a tempo suited to a waltz. Although my niece liked nightclubs filled with vibrations from thumping base drums tracks, her ballroom dancing skills are good. Edie paid for her to attend dancing classes which she kept going to for a while, which we looked upon as a triumph. I think she enjoyed them, but the peer pressure pulled her away from what was deemed to be old style dancing.

We enjoyed the coffee and ordered another bottle of white wine which was not the best idea, but it would have been rude not to try the different varieties from the vineyards of Tuscany.

The different shades of orange framed the spectacular sunset and illuminated Florence's red rooftops.

"Who've you seen?" I asked my niece.

"No one!" she replied defensively.

"Don't try and pull the wool over my eyes. One, because I'm too old and two, because it is far too hot for a woollen hat!"

"You're so funny. Not!" came the reply as her pupils dilated and eyelids fluttered like the fast shutter speed of a camera with a long-focus lens, as used by the paparazzi.

Out of the corner of my eye, I first glimpsed the focus of her attention. A stereotypical, tall, dark, handsome stranger. His shiny, shoulder length, jet black hair with a hint of a wave rested on a crisp white cotton shirt – the same as all the other members of the band.

I looked at my niece with a mischievous grin and said, "quick! Think of a song. He's asking for requests."

"Don't be silly," my niece replied. "He's going to ask me to dance. It's obvious!" She flicked her hair aside – proud as a peacock.

Before we had the chance to take a breath, Edie was dancing with him.

"What!?!" My niece protested boldly and a little too loudly.

"Never mind," I said. "The drummer is looking for a dance partner."

"Please, aunty! You've had way too much wine. He's old enough to be my dad and mum is old enough to be the guitarist's grandmother!"

"You can be so cruel at times," I reprimanded my niece.

"I am not cruel, just totally embarrassed."

"Totally jealous?" I teased my niece who I love dearly. She and her brother have ridden the storm of divorce without too much 'see and hear' sickness. Some children, never mind their age, are exposed to unwarranted amounts of acrimonious behaviour. Children are weaponised even more than property. In retrospect the arguments were rarely linked to custody because Tarquin did not have time to spend with his children. Their time together was brief with a long gap between each '*meeting*' as he referred to the arrangements. And Tarquin, or more accurately – his new wife wanted a new home, so he was not too troubled with leaving Edie to live in their house. He was only concerned about the equity accrued in the property but knew he did not have a leg to stand on with regards claiming his share due to the lack of child maintenance. Also, Edie could claim compensation for the loss of earnings and pension contributions because all her time and energy was invested in his rise to be the top sales negotiator in the branch and region, leading to promotion to Director. Tarquin knew but would not admit, his father-in-law pointed potential clients towards his path to success.

My niece stormed off to the toilet and was in such a 'huff' she left her handbag on the table. I took her mobile out of the bag, switched it off and put it at the bottom of my rucksack – she had no chance of finding it in there. The expected meltdown ensued, and I asked Jo to keep her voice down. "Please, Jo!" I pleaded with an agitated niece who was literally ready to explode. "Sit down and I'll order you a cocktail."

"Cheers," the feeble response was followed with an earnest request. "I need to send the Assistant Director a message. I forgot to put the spare costumes in the correct wardrobe. He's stressed to the limit. He will blow a gasket. He already has high blood pressure."

"My blood pressure has increased just listening to that work of fiction," I said. "Your mobile is safe; don't worry! It's having some time out. I switched it off, so we do not have to listen to the incessant notification bell. Once your mum has finished the dance or hopefully dances with the extremely handsome young man; your mobile will be returned."

"Aunty, you can be so patronising at times! You spoke to me with more respect when I was five. Enough of this nonsense. I need a cigarette. Suppose you have taken them as well?"

"No," I replied slowly. "You cannot take photos of your mum and put them on Facebook using your lighter and cigarettes. You'll probably have to go downstairs or hang off the side of the balcony. This is all non-smoking now."

"Ha! Ha! See you've have had more wine for Dutch courage?" My niece stomped loudly as she went to the lift. I accepted her tantrums. She should have outgrown them; however, we all have our breaking points. Jo has a shorter fuse than her brother. The impact of the divorce hit her the hardest. She felt each tremor and absorbed all the blows for a relatively long time, but it is all coming to the surface. I tolerate her outbursts however will not be used as a punch bag and have made that abundantly clear to her. We know we love each other deeply. The core thread is stretched and frayed but in faith too strong to snap.

Edie floated back to the table. Her dance partner held out her chair and said, "Grazie Signorina." His smile would melt a block of ice – a solid block of ice in the chest freezer.

"You, okay?" I asked.

"Yeah, sure," she replied. "Is there any more wine left?"

"I'll order another bottle. Think you may need another glass to calm your nerves." Edie's hands were shaking, not out of fear but from feeling alive again. Her flushed cheeks matched the burning colours intertwined in the remnants of the sun set.

"Where is Jo?" Edie's question was topped with a layer of guilt.

"Miss huffy pants has gone to have a cigarette."

Edie smiled and said, "she promised to give up."

"I promised to give up chocolate last week! We've got a lot in common."

"Hope she is alright?" Edie voiced her concern. "She'll probably go to a night club."

"Not without her mobile." I reached into my rucksack

"What did you do that for?" Edie protested. "She needs it for work!"

I retaliated, "she needs it to take photos to share with *'Uncle Tom Cobley and all.'* That was your private moment in time – not one to be trending on Twitter. I have only had it for ten minutes. I do not think the theatre will collapse. They have a super-efficient production team."

The waiter came to the table with an ice-bucket cradling a bottle of Champagne. "Sorry," I said. "I think you have the wrong table. We ordered a bottle of wine?"

"Scusi, Signorina," the polished waiter proffered an explanation. "A gift from Signor Domenico Giardino – the guitar player – in the band. Would you like to try the Cuvée Rosé – Chardonnay?"

"Sorry. No." I flustered a response. "We are surprised. Scusi. A nice surprise. Can we cancel the order for wine? Too much in one evening. I will pay if you have opened the bottle."

"Please do not worry Signorina. No extra cost – all paid. I will bring champagne glasses. Two?"

"Three please," I replied and whispered to Edie, "best not leave out Miss Super Busy or she will throw all her toys out of the pram!"

The smell of nicotine preceded the return of my niece. "Have you been talking about me?"

"Nope!" I replied.

"Champagne!" Jo expressed her surprise. "Really pushing the boat out tonight, aunty."

"Don't thank me," I said. "A gift from an admirer," I turned my line of sight to the guitarist, and he smiled again which made me shudder with exhilaration.

"Wow! Super handsome and super rich!" My niece declared loudly. "Don't let that one go, mum!"

I kicked my niece's ankle. "OUCH!" she shrieked.

"Sorry," I said. "Touch of cramp in my toes. Before you ask, here's your mobile."

"Thank you," my niece said before making an announcement. "I must reply to Giuseppe's message. How embarrassing! I had to write down my mobile number. I don't think he understands my accent. Who doesn't have their mobile with them? Felt like a golden oldie!"

"Who is Giuseppe?" Edie asked.

"Oh, he's invited me to a traditional bar – away from the centre and all the touristy places."

"You've only just met him?" The angst in Edie's voice heightened, but she fell into the trap.

"Yes," her daughter replied. "He's my holiday romance – same as you but my one's older!"

I glared at my niece. She is so infuriating at times and still goes through phases of blaming her mum for the divorce. Unfortunately, she has had weak moments of absorbing the spin from Tarquin. After all he is her dad and can play the emotional hand of cards which does not work with Sebastian. Tarquin's coercive behaviour would break into the strongest boundary wall especially when Jo was being bullied at school and suffering from a roller coaster of hormones.

The evening in La Terrazza Brunelleschi ended with the band playing the romantic song Firenze sogna (Florence dreams)

Edie and Domenico moved slowly in harmony; mesmerised by the lyrics. They did not notice they were the only couple on the dance floor. I am not sure they even knew the day nor month. My soft smile masked a slither of envy but it was also a broadcast of relief when I opened the napkin that Jo shoved in my hand. The eyeliner smudged the words, but I could read. "Sorry. Won't be long! In bar opposite hotel."

My trip to Florence in 2010 was lovely. Edie's experience in Florence was life changing.

***

CHAPTER 8

Feeble beeping from the tatty mobile phone cover prompted the withdrawal from an entanglement of clutter in my wardrobe.

"Hello," I stuttered. Dust lodged in my throat and the strain in my voice represented the stress stirring in my stomach.

"Mary! How are you?"

"Yeah, okay." My confused tone haltered the flow of conversation.

"Good! Good!" came the synthetic hyper response. The awkward silence precipitated the louder announcement: "Tarquin here! You know, Tarquin – the solution to all your problems! The only Estate Agent you need to know!"

"Oh yes.," I replied and then bit my lip to stop the frustration from boiling over. "Is there any news," I asked.

"Only good news from me. You know that! Group of potential buyers will be around at five. That's okay, isn't it?"

"Five!" I exclaimed. "It's four-thirty! I believe in miracles, but I can't get ready and clean all the boxes out of the way in thirty minutes! Owen promised all viewings would be confirmed in an e-mail?"

"Well, I don't have access to his e-mails. He runs his own private empire." The resentment in Tarquin's voice was filled with anger. Although Tarquin's usual sales patter drives me to distraction – I sense different elements; doubt and desperation which are far from usual.

"I'll have to change the appointments!" His guilt-ridden statement hung in the air.

"I did not have an appointment to change!" I retorted.

"You'll probably lose out on a quick sale. You're not making it easy for me."

I took a deep breath and forcefully stopped the words, balancing on my lips, to tumble out. My self-censorship prevented an unnecessary, fruitless, exchange of curt words. I do suffer from '*foot-in-mouth*' disease however on this occasion the filter kicked in because my '*worry rucksack*' was full to the brim with unresolved issues.

"How many of them?" I asked wearily.

Tarquin knew he had me on the ropes. "Expecting four but if Owen gets any walk-ins, I'll squeeze them in. What if we make it five-thirty? I can hold them for a while?"

I was not sure where Tarquin was going to hold them?

"Yes, alright," I said impatiently topped with a layer of anxiety.

"You're a star!" Tarquin claimed his victory and earnestly instructed, "remember, sparkling clean and minimalist. Help me out. Give me something to work with."

Before I had the chance to reply, Tarquin had ended the call and I had to start hiding items in cupboards, and put piles of clothes, destined for the charity shop, in the shared hall. There was not time to hoover so used a strong yard brush to gather dust, strands of hair and scraps from cardboard boxes. I fixed a bigger and bolder sign on the blind in the bathroom and left the doors of the hall cupboards open to save the strain on the hinges. The tea stain clung onto the scratched sink. There was no time to use the amount of spray required and did not have enough scouring pads. The oven had been professionally cleaned which was a relief. I opened the door and quickly removed the tin foil which had remnants of the fish fingers and French fries from the previous evening. The smell was not too bad. It was a mild evening so the windows could be open slightly, but I was weary of the wasps which were frequent visitors.

"Hello! Hello!" Tarquin called out. I did not wait for the typical script and did not need to be informed of the Estate Agent he represented.

"Mary! How are you?" Tarquin went through his pre-scripted lines. "We won't take long, will we?" Tarquin looked at the four potential buyers. They nodded obediently and he called out, "guys, we need to take our shoes off. Just leave them in the hall – no one will take them!"

"I hope no one trips over them," I thought.

The two giggly sisters were in the group. "Hello," they shrilled together. "Thank you so much for letting us come back. We are so grateful! You must be super busy, packing?"

"Yes," I replied tentatively, worried that Tarquin had set them up to pile the pressure on me. "De-cluttering is the priority, hence all the bags in the hall."

The taller sister nudged her sibling and teased, "she's still de-cluttering her make up. Wants to splash the cash on hottest brands and get fit and ready for summer hols in Ibiza."

"Thought you ladies would be going to Mallorca?" Tarquin interrupted with a lecherous grin. The perplexed look on my face ignited Tarquin's sarcasm. "Mary, let me explain. The final of Love Island? You know, the TV show? The final is on Monday. That's right isn't ladies?"

"Yes," they giggled. The petite sister said dreamily, "I'm still thinking about Brad Pitt at Wimbledon. How can anyone look so cool eating crisps?"

"I was in the Royal Box," Tarquin boasted. "Did you see me?"

"No!" The sisters replied dismissively and continued their conversation about "game, set and match to Brad."

I sniggered and went to the bathroom to check on the blind. The same questions ensued, and the frustration was visible when I could not provide details of a moving date or any progress on my new home. A few wasps came in to see their prospective flat mates.

"Oooh! We don't like wasps!" the giggly sisters screeched.

"Don't worry ladies," Tarquin said. "The management company are planning to cut back the trees in October. All the issues will be resolved."

I shook my head slowly and went to the front door because I wanted to apologise to my neighbour who was returning from work. She was understanding but it did concern me how long the tolerance of all my neighbours would last.

"Mary!" Tarquin continued with his attention seeking communication. That man will be here in ten."

"What man?" I asked. "And, sorry, what is ten?"

"You know, that one who was late to the party, on the open day? He'll be here in ten minutes?" Tarquin explained patronisingly. "He kept staring at you. Guessing he knows you? Just to be clear, there's no *mates rates*. I'm not reducing my commission for a blast from the past."

"Wouldn't dream of depriving you of your precious commission, Tarquin. You have a family to support!" My catty comment came to an abrupt halt. It was pointless prodding the bear.

The door buzzer diverted my attention. "Yes, please come up. The flat has not moved!" I immediately regretted my clumsy attempt at humour.

My gaze locked into his eyes and the surrounding sound faded. When the past stares you directly in the face the passage of time zooms past: different strings of time run in parallel. The thin thread connected the two dimensions.

"OKAY GUYS!" Tarquin shouted. "Need to go!" He herded his flock of potential buyers in a vigorous manner. "I've got another property to show you – brand new block at the end of the road. The show home will be closing soon. They're keeping it open as a favour – specially for you."

"Bye, Bye," the giggly sisters reached out to give me a hug. "Lovely to see you again. We'll bring a bottle of Prosecco the next time!"

"That sounds a nice idea," I replied.

The giggly sisters looked at the gentleman and said, "we know you! We saw you outside last time – what did Tarquin call it?"

"Super Saturday, "I whispered and cringed at the thought of the description.

"Wow! We can all have a party here next time," said the giggly sisters. They roared with laughter and wobbled on their stilettos.

"Sorry, buddy!" Tarquin said. "I can't leave you here on your own. I trust you 100% but can't say the same for Mary!" Tarquin chortled at his own joke which did not resonate with the recipients. "We'll have to make another appointment. When you've sorted out how to plan your route here?"

Neil Bach nodded in compliance and smiled reassuringly.

"Must Dash!" Tarquin announced his departure. All my neighbours must have heard him and shared the same sense of relief. He continued as he leaped down the stairs, "wasted minutes means wasted money. Time is money!"

***

CHAPTER 9

"DELIVERY!"

"Where's your keys?" I asked through my locked front door.

"At the bottom of my bag!" Nicola replied exasperated after carrying two bags of groceries up the stairs because the lift had broken down again.

"Why didn't you call me? "I said, "I could've come down to help you carry the bags."

"You'll scare the neighbours in those PJs," Nicola quipped. "Have you packed your hairbrush already?"

"Ha! Ha!" I groaned. "I was just about to get into the shower. I mean scramble over the side of the bath. Thought you were coming later when Andy's watching cricket in the pub.?"

"Change of plan. Andy is organising a secret for my birthday and wants me out of the way."

"Secret? Andy organising?" I teased, "are you sure you've taken your multi-vitamin tablets?"

"Yes. Thank you very much," came the indignant reply. "When I say secret, it is not really a secret. He's booking the church hall for my birthday party."

"Okay, Miss Nosey. How did you find out?" I asked: intrigued and in awe of her detective skills.

"The church administrator called the landline and asked for a deposit."

"Oh, no!" I tried not to laugh. "What did you say?"

"I told her to call Andy's mobile. And I promised I'd forget her call."

"Poor bloke," I empathised. "He tries his best and gets caught in the act."

"Tea and Toast?" Nicola asked.

"Great, thanks," I replied from the bathroom. Be out in a minute.

"You've got strawberry jam!" I squealed with delight.

"Can't say I don't spoil you."

I moved the clean laundry pile from the cosy armchair, "you sit here; I'll get a blanket and sit on the floor."

"You sure you'll get up again?" came the cheeky reply.

"I'm ignoring it! I'm ignoring it!" I covered my ears with a determination not to let Nicola wind me up.

Nicola laughed. "So, how are you getting on?" You've told Tarquin, no viewings today?"

"Yes, I did. Absolutely no viewings today. Can't have open days every Saturday. I'm worn out and the neighbours must be fed up with his shouting "

"Good!" Nicola replied emphatically and continued, "I've put your shopping away."

"I could've ordered online," I replied with a sense of guilt because Nicola has enough to do.

"Really?" Nicola smirked. "I dread to think what you would've ended up with!"

"So rude!" I chuckled. "Jo showed me what to do about five or six times! When she lost her temper, Sebastian taught me in one relaxed lesson via zoom."

"My, my," Nicola replied mockingly, "you are becoming a Miss Techie."

"Leave me to have my toast and enjoy dropping crumbs over this worn-out old carpet! "I said.

"It'll go nicely with the tea stain," Nicola said. "It doesn't matter; the new owners will modernise the place?"

"Don't you start!" I replied. "I've had Tarquin and potential buyers telling me how they are going to redecorate and bring it up to modern style. They think I live in a vintage museum. And to top it off; Tarquin wants to show a minimalist style. What's that?"

"He might as well forget that approach," Nicola said. "It'll take you to this time next year to declutter and move all these boxes."

"No. That's not true," I replied defensively. "I've brought two bags of clothes to the charity shop and the recycling company are coming next week to take away some of the boxes in the garage.

"Okay, that's progress, but why the snail pace?" Nicola's probing question hit the bullseye.

"I'm exhausted," I sighed and rubbed my forehead. "Don't really know what to do and keep finding cards and gifts, mum and dad gave me and can't throw them away. I'm still clinging on to the Father's Day card I bought for dad this year. And can't get Tarquin's ridiculous catch phrases out my head; and can't stand it when he's telling bear faced lies about the management agent planning repairs, when they've already told us they haven't got the budget to carry out any more major repairs this year."

"Lies?" Nicola challenged me to think about the accusation, "or a puffed up Pollyana?"

I smiled and said, "now I won't be able to get that image out of my head. Tarquin's alright if you can cut out the noise pollution."

"You don't have to put up with all the nonsense," Nicola said. "There are plenty of Estate Agents in the sea and they won't charge that much more?" He's already done a lot of damage to your family. Don't let him walk all over you!"

"I know, I know," I sighed. "There's no doubt he'll get rid of the flat It's just the in between stage that will make me pull my hair out! But there is something odd going on: he's got the old sales pitch, but he really sounds desperate? It all seems a bit strange."

"He's not top dog anymore," Nicola replied knowingly. "The website shows Quenton Seal is the manager, and Tarquin is just part of the sales team – no official title."

"Not sure what's going on, but don't want him to go bankrupt. He'll sell Jo's flat in a blink of an eye if he needs to raise money. When he sells this flat, it will help; but won't solve all his problems."

"At that rate he'll be pushing everyone through the door." Nicola said and followed up with a question, "has he found anyone vaguely interested in the flat?"

"There is a few," I replied. "The girl who came with her parents seems to be ideal, well her mum thinks she is. The giggly sisters have been here twice and not sure if they're here for something to do. Tarquin would show them around every day. A few other stragglers and then the man who has been here twice – brief viewings; so, we're hoping to have more time when he returns on his own."

"Mary! I know you're tired but don't let strange men walk around your flat when you're on your own."

"Astonishingly, he's not strange!" I said waiting for the tirade of questions.

"What do you mean he's not strange?" Nicola asked with a sense of urgency. "Do you need another cup of tea – more caffeine might make you speak sense!"

"It's Neil!"

"Neil who?" Nicola replied impatiently.

"Bach," I replied tentatively and then whispered with emotion etched on my face, "Neil Bach!"

"Shut the door!" Nicola's loud reply bounced off the window.

"I wish I had," I replied. "But Tarquin ushers everyone in at such a speed!"

"Are you sure it's Neil? Your Neil?" Nicola asked awkwardly.

"Yes. Sure," I responded. "As Tarquin would say, 110%!"

"Did Tarquin recognise him?"

"Don't think so. Even if he did, it's no interest to him. He wants commission not my back story. Tarquin has told Neil; it's not a private sale. All offers must go through Dale Estate Agents, so I am guessing he thinks something is different but he's not going to waste his time trying to find out."

"My goodness," Nicola's voice waivered. "How on earth did he know where you live? He mentioned to Andy he is looking for a new flat, but he did not put two and two together. Knowing Andy, he'll make it to be five anyway! I know their best friends, but Andy would not have told him where you live – you know that don't you?"

"Yes," I responded reassuringly, "I am cynical, but I trust you two oldies."

"I'll tell Andy to tell Neil to stop buying the flat." Nicola said with a sense of urgency.

"What?" I exclaimed. "It's a free market! If he wants to buy the flat and is willing to pay top dollar – let him fill his boots."

"Andy told him about going to your dad's funeral, so I suppose he came to look in the area. Neil lives in Rainham. He has gone to a lot of trouble to find you, seeing you're not on socials."

"I wonder what is going on in his life to cause him to buy a flat – it's far too small for a family?" I said – fishing for information and Nicola read me like a book.

"Andy mentioned Neil and his wife have been going through a rocky patch. You know, Andy, he doesn't gossip but we were trying to think of where to go for my birthday and who to invite. When I mentioned, Neil and Caroline and the children, Andy didn't reply, so I knew something wasn't right. I am guessing he will invite them to my, not so secret, birthday party. I cannot uninvite Neil!"

"Absolutely not!" I said sharply. "Andy and Neil have been friends since the dinosaurs roamed the earth. Well, not that long but not far off. Anyway, I haven't got an invitation to your birthday party."

"This is your invitation," Nicola said with a smile. "You're going!"

"That's sorted then!" I replied. "Thank you to my diary secretary."

"You're most welcome," Nicola laughed but her serious expression pre-warned for the next piece of advice. "Don't get your hopes up. I doubt he will leave her. He never wanted to leave you. You know that – deep down? It was too much for him and you. He didn't have the maturity to deal with it – talk to you and you were too stubborn to listen or to compromise. I'm forewarning you not to read too much into this bizarre twist of fate. We can all dream of the four of us going out together again for pub lunches and playing darts, but we must face reality. And you are in a vulnerable state. It's not the best time to get involved emotionally."

"I'm not dreaming," I replied. "I'm moving. Probably will be best to go abroad. Get away. Make a fresh start. That's what I want to do."

"Really?" asked Nicola with an insightful stare into my crumpled face.

***

Nicola helped pack boxes and took clothes for the charity shop just in case I changed my mind. I sat in the cosy armchair with a fresh supply of toast and a porridge in a pot. A cooked meal was not appealing. I was confused and extremely tired. The last person I expected to walk through my door was Neil Bach. I wondered if he genuinely wanted to buy the flat or just wanted to reconnect with me. Nicola's warning rattled around my head, but my heart was racing in a different direction.

The end of my relationship with Neil was incredibly sad and in retrospect an incredible waste. When the cracks started to show the criticism intensified in the office. There were opposing camps – blaming each other for the demise of the relationship which almost had a celebrity status. Initially, I think it was because we were genuinely happy, and the simplicity intrigued some. Why was I happy not going to expensive restaurants and having champagne? Neil did not buy long stem red roses – he didn't have to. The genuine generous gestures of surreptitiously leaving small bags of salted peanuts on my desk, meant so much more than empty gestures to get the attention of others. The coach trips in freezing temperatures and worn-out seats meant the world to us. Our colleagues could not get to grips with how content we were. I remember standing in a pub in Covent Garden: a night out for a colleague emigrating to Australia. Neil was wearing his baggy blue jumper, and I was wearing a black polyester dress which looked similar to velvet, at a certain angle in the dimmed light. Warren was overjoyed about returning home. He had made every effort to guard us from the disparaging remarks in the office. He was a free spirit, and we joined in singing, "Down Under" by Men At Work before his final departure. Without Warren we were more vulnerable to negative comments. This was one factor which toppled our secure structure.

My team leader Nigel Peek, instigated insults via his on/off girlfriend Janette. When she felt insecure and envious of our steadfast commitment, we were good target practice for her bitter arrows. Janette openly flirted with Neil. I tried to laugh but when she sat on his desk with her mini skirt no longer visible – the humiliation shattered my self-confidence. Neil did not instigate the behaviour, but he was a young man – how could he push Janette off the desk in front of his colleagues especially the men who were extremely jealous. The next morning, I sat at my desk with red puffy eyes and gave the excuse that I had an allergic reaction to my new make-up. The stinging sensation in my eyes was as sharp as the tear in my heart. After such incidents in the office, I would withdraw and keep a distance from Neil. He almost pleaded with me to go to lunch. Andy's approach was typical Andy, "nothing that a pie and chips and a game of darts can't sort out!" I did not see the funny side. Neil accepted Andy's invitation – anything to alleviate the stress which was piling up.

Neil's mother did not trust me from day one. We tried to do the false respectful act for Neil's sake however the friction was palpable. The overtly polite and passive aggressive comments became increasingly strained therefore we purposefully lengthened the gaps between each meeting. The distance resulted in resentment. The topic of a working-class lifestyle raised its head above the level of reasonability. I never found the root cause of this conflict. Mum and dad provided us with a comfortable life because of their hard work and the same applied to grandpa and grandma. I was not born with a silver spoon in my mouth, nor do I think anyone could have put us in the upper-class category. And

I was not sure how Neil's mother categorised the different classes:-I sensed there was inverted snobbery at play. She did not want Neil to buy a house – "too pretentious." A two-bedroom flat – "too excessive." A one-bedroom flat – "would suffice." Neil's older brother had lost money on foolish choices in relation to property, women, and gambling. Loans were granted to him from the bank of mum and dad, but he defaulted on the repayments. Neil bore the brunt of the fallout from the antics of his brother.

During our years together, we kept our outgoings within budget and saved regularly. We felt incredibly grown up when we opened our joint building society account. Neil's mother voiced her concern and stipulated that there had to be two signatures before a withdrawal is authorised. At each turn I thought Neil's mother would soften her edges but the longer we stayed together the more entrenched she became in finding faults and going out of her way to cause friction.

Our holiday destinations were not exotic in comparison to our colleagues. Trips to the seaside were our favourite. Ranging from Margate to Morecombe, Leysdown to Lyme Regis, Brighton to Bournemouth – we stayed in Bed & Breakfasts and caravans. The weekends away with Nicola and Andy were memorable and fun. Andy was delighted to have a "*bodyguard*" as he called it when he had crossed words with Nicola. When Andy and Neil conveniently booked a hotel near a football ground, Nicola and me enjoyed our "girlie time." Chatting about everything and nothing. When I started talking about work, Nicola abruptly ended the conversation, and I got the silent treatment until we could establish common ground again. "I'm doing it for your own good," she used to say. And then divulged too much information even for a close friend, "do you know he even talks about work in bed?! How romantic! Can just hear it now, '*Romeo, Romeo, where for art thou Claim Payments*!?!' Unfortunately, she continued, fuelled by another wine spritzer, "do you know, he can't even concentrate on, you know?"

"Enough!" I exclaimed. "Stop! You'd be really angry if Andy was divulging your bedtime behaviour?"

"Don't be silly," Nicola said. "Andy only talks about darts and football – he doesn't have the time to fit in any details about bedtime secrets."

Nicola and me enjoyed our lunch times with 'the boys' as we called them: Andy and Neil. Two grown men who were not bothered by the banter and did not have to prove their masculinity. Water off a duck's back. They played darts and occasionally let us join in but gave the customers in the pub a public warning before the start of the game – much to the hilarity of the bar staff. On one occasion, Nicola told Andy where she will be throwing her dart. She did not whisper her proposed target but delivered the proclamation to the other customers.

I was never comfortable when Neil stayed at mum and dad's home. The spare guest room – Edie's old bedroom was prepared with the same level of diligence as that used in top notch hotels. Mum made sure everything was in order. But we were young and very much in love – temptation took hold sometimes. Even though mum and dad were modern and accepting; it did not feel right especially when they were in the house. They just wanted us to be happy and have the time to save for our home. Grandma and grandpa offered to loan us the deposit for a house, but Neil refused, politely. He could not cope with the backlash from his mother and upon reflection maybe it was a sign he did not want to live with me. So, we continued our quest to save as much as practical.

The pressure eased when mum and dad went on holiday. We play acted at being the owner of my parents' house which seemed fun at the beginning and even felt cosy, but doubt crept in slowly but surely. Neil's parents enjoyed staying in Tenerife during the winter – their friend had a time share apartment. I am not sure how this fitted in with the *'working class lifestyle'* but it was at the gift of their friend until he retired and then their winter arrangements would have to change. Neil's brother moved in with his ex-wife again, so we had Neil's home to ourselves for lengthy periods of time. He was more at ease in the two-bedroom maisonette. I did not blame him because he had lived there all his life. The commute to work was longer but I used to fall asleep on his shoulder whilst he read the sports pages of the Daily Mirror. It was nice but the depth of our emotional connection was a world away from our time on the winter coaches.

The dam burst during our holiday to Halkidiki in Greece during the summer of 1986. The cost of the holiday was over our usual budget, but I was exasperated at watching colleagues returning from Mediterranean holidays with tans and tales of exploring landscapes and meeting foreign waiters – if the truth be known. We thought we would *'splash out'* on one summer holiday abroad but sadly it dampened the remaining fire between us. Neil projected his unhappiness on beach bikini babes, and I projected my frustration on learning Zorba the Greek dance with too much enthusiasm – closely following Takis Kyriakous, the dance teacher. Both of us made fruitless liaisons. We were faithful in body, but our minds drifted to darker places. We were two different people looking to follow different paths in the future. Hindsight is a wonderful thing – I do wonder if we would have been better off going on separate holidays and then re-grouping when we returned. You cannot keep driving a car on two flat tyres. Eventually the suspension and steering system will be damaged: not to mention the substantial risk of a head on collision and the fallout from the accident.

Janette was the leader of the gang who thrived on our downfall. The name of Mick Fuller was dug up and speedily buried again when my manager overheard the gossipy group. Rumours spread like wildfire – someone had photos of Mick and me in The Ship and Compass.

The manager tolerated banter about Neil and me, but this was way over the boundary wall. Janette was requested to attend a meeting with Sue Hamilton, the manager of Personnel (Human Resources) and given a warning. She left the company soon after the incident: no photos were presented for public viewing, and no evidence surfaced in relation to Janette's friendship with Chris Reed, who had recently been promoted to the position of Director of Accounts.

Neil never asked about my past and I respected the privacy of his past. I assumed someone in the office would have been only too delighted to inform Neil of my role as a mistress. It was another thorn in our side which tore into the flesh of our hearts.

After the official split from Neil, I continued working in Britus Assurance Company. We were distantly polite. Exchanged a few verbal pleasantries but overheard a lot more. And as much as I knew listening to his conversations would hurt – the intense need to find out what he was doing continued.

Thankfully, neither of us had a dalliance with another colleague on the rebound. We had relationships but they were with 'outsiders.'

Nicola and Andy were in unenviable positions. Although Andy empathised with my sadness, he was extremely protective about Neil. One aspect in his life where he would not back down. And one of the few times when Nicola knew not to push him. Andy was relieved when Neil found a new relationship with Caroline Cavin. Andy did not connect with her as much as he did with me. There was the age gap and the different backgrounds. She was more serious than me and had little interest in football and most definitely would not play darts. But she had her own house and was a stable influence, in the first half of their relationship. She had two children from her previous marriage which did not trouble Neil; so, he said. Andy worried because he knew Neil would like to be a dad – take his boys to football with Uncle Andy; but Nicola tried to convince him that Caroline could still have children if that is what they both genuinely wanted. Nicola had doubts if they were on the same page. Caroline offered regimented routine and no complex decisions about where to live and choice of house. All aspects were in place – Neil just had to step in line.

I stayed in my job as long as possible. My emotional resilience subsided in 1987. There was a strong bond to my first full time employer, but I had to make a fresh start. Saying farewell was not easy at all. Nicola did not want me to leave but did not want me to be in the shadow of my past. Although Neil and me had separate lives there was a surreal comfort from seeing him in the office. Did I hope there would be a momentous reconciliation?

On the surface – maybe.

Deep down – definitely.

***

CHAPTER 10

"Looks so different!" My observation was met a sharp retort.

"I should hope so after forty-three years. Surprise the place is still standing," Nicola replied.

"It looks much bigger," my assessment continued of a venue which played a significant role in our past.

"Probably, because it's not filled with cigarette smoke!" said Nicola.

"I quite miss those days; glass in one hand, cigarette in the other!" I reflected on a Hollywood image not reality.

"You obviously don't remember the stale smell of nicotine on your clothes, and hair, and breath!" Nicola complained from the point of view of a non-smoker.

"It was fine, we both smoked!" The awkward pause prompted Nicola into action mode; she knew the "we" meant Neil and me; four decades had passed but I was still in relationship with Neil.

"Have you seen the price of the jacket potato? Look at the one over there – only has a sprinkle of grated cheese on top." Nicola complained.

"Order what you like," I said. "It's your early birthday treat. I do not want to intrude on your '*not*' a surprise birthday party on Saturday."

"Has Andy sent you an invitation?" Nicola asked eagerly.

"Now that would be telling!" I teased.

"Don't be so silly!" Nicola retorted. "I just want to make sure Andy has sent invitations otherwise there will be just, him, me and you on the dance floor!"

"And my '*plus one*'" I replied.

"Who?" asked Nicola.

"Andy included my name and '*plus one*'" I said.

"He's such a numpty!" Nicola groaned. "He should've put '*and guest.*'

"Don't complain," I jumped to Andy's defence. "At least he's sent out invitations which is better than most men would do. They would send group message things. There would be no personal touch."

"I think you mean, WhatsApp groups?" Nicola mocked my lack of comprehension or connection with social media. "Don't worry he has a message group thingy for my party."

"How do you know?" I asked.

"It's my job to know!" Nicola grinned. "Other than that, Andy asked me to change the security settings on his mobile and there so happened to be a message from the group!"

"Honestly, poor Andy," I exclaimed. "It must be like living with Miss Marple."

"How rude!" Nicola giggled. "I do not look anything like Miss Marple; I had my highlights done last week, with a few more autumnal shades that you have not noticed yet!"

"Stop fishing for compliments," I said, "and select something from the menu before the bar closes."

"Now, you really are, showing your age," Nicola laughed. "The pubs don't shut in the afternoon like they used to when we worked here."

"No, I'm talking about closing time, this evening, at the rate you are going!" I said.

"Okay, Miss Tetchy," Nicola quipped and placed an order for quiche and chips.

We found a table in the corner where the dartboard used to be and admired the new carpet free from cigarette burns.

"These portions wouldn't feed the pigeons!" Nicola moaned.

"You need fewer calories so you can get into your dress on Saturday!" I chortled.

"Cheek!" Nicola frowned. "We're supposed to be having a girlie lunch and a stroll down memory lane not attending weight watchers. It's turning into an O.A.P. afternoon snack."

"Afternoon nap!" I replied. "Would go down a treat!"

"Just listen to the pair of us," Nicola chuckled. "Bit different from 1980s?"

"Certainly are," I said.

***

I offered to buy Nicola a white wine spritzer for old times' sake, but she reeled back at the price, so we calculated it to be more cost effective to buy a bottle of prosecco.

Our voices were not drowned out by catchy Christmas songs but the sound of the past echoed through my mind. I could see Neil squashed in the corner by the window. His fresh face had not been damaged by the pollution of pressure from long hours in the office or the pain of heart break. My bubbly optimism and revitalisation after the shaky start at Britus Assurance Company rose above the cigarette smoke. Looking through rose-tinted glasses, it was young love, but it was simply love. No deception – no ulterior motive – no planning. Simply love.

***

"Do you want a dessert?" I asked.

"Not at these prices!" Nicola snapped. "I'll get a bar of chocolate at the station."

"Hope you're less moody on Saturday," I said. "You'll have to find your happy face."

"Very funny!" Nicola replied.

"Are Nicholas and Rose going?" I asked

"They better!" Nicola quipped. "And they won't miss the opportunity to remind their mother how old she is. I'm sure Rose has ordered the biggest numbered balloons possible just to make sure everyone knows I am sixty! How did that happen? I want to be sixteen again!"

"No you don't! "I said. "Would you seriously want all our antics plastered over the internet?!"

"No, thank you!" Nicola replied. "Bad enough when we got the photos developed at Boots." She paused and then said, "Hold on a minute, our antics? I went out with Andy – don't think that would make it into the gossip magazines! Your antics were a lot more colourful!"

"Unfortunately, they were when I started work. Why didn't you save me?" I pleaded.

"Because I didn't know you! Duh!" Nicola chuckled. A seriousness took over her face and a sensitivity filled her voice. "We were all right – four of us together? Weren't we?"

"Yep," I sighed. "Alright and happy."

Nicola saw the tears well up in my eyes and burst into party planning mode. "Hope he's ordered enough food and remembered Rose is a vegetarian.

"It'll be alright on the night," I said. "Andy has it all in hand. Well, if he doesn't – a quick trip down to Sainsbury's should sort it all out. But we can't let you go in your finery. Have you bought a new dress?"

"No!" Nicola retorted. "Keep up! How can I buy a new party dress for a party that I am not supposed to know about? I bought Rose a new outfit which she hastily returned.

She'll find something more fashionable, and we are saying it is for her 30th birthday."

"Has she made up her mind what she wants to do?" I asked

"No, don't be silly," Nicola replied in the usual frustrated tone with regards her daughter. "The latest is that she wants to go trekking. Said something about going to Kilimanjaro with her work colleagues! She's asked if we'll look after Christine. Andy loves spoiling his granddaughter at every chance he gets so it will work out for the best."

"Blimey, that's a bit different from a party in a church hall. I'll have a chat with Rose on Saturday –see if she needs a new pair of hiking boots! It'll be nice to catch up. In the meantime, let's go to Covent Garden and I'll buy you a dress for your birthday. That should sort that bit of the jigsaw out. And we can make sure it's 1980's style – nice big shoulder pads and gold lamé."

"Little black dress is more my style," Nicola replied. "And I don't want to clash with your outfit!"

***

"Show me your surprised face," I said.

Nicola gave a cheesy grin.

"No!" I reprimanded my best friend who was getting ready for her '*not*' surprise birthday party. "You can do better than that. Think of Andy who has been trying his best to organise a party – not his strongest skill, to put it mildly."

"Don't feel too sorry for him; Nicholas and Christine have been with him this afternoon," Nicola replied as she looked in the mirror to master her faked shock face.

"Christine will take charge," I said, "knowing Andy."

"Too right," Nicola pondered. "He dotes on his

186

granddaughter: she has a new dress but that is not out of the ordinary, we both love buying her clothes and she is so grateful. I am thankful Andy is not great at clothes shopping online otherwise we would have to buy Christine another wardrobe. He orders gift vouchers for her, and then we have a shopping hour once she has completed all her homework and household chores."

"I'll have to invite Christine for afternoon tea and a clean," I joked.

"It would have to be a sleepover," Nicola quipped. "Couldn't get your flat clean in an afternoon."

"If you weren't my best friend, I'd storm out!" I pouted and tried not to burst out laughing. "Go on then," Nicola teased, "see if I care? Leaving me alone to complete my impossible make over for my birthday party, about which I do not know."

I giggled and continued to pull Nicola's dress into shape.

"No doubt Nicholas will be working in the corner," Nicola anticipated the stance of her oldest and favourite child. "Betty and the boys will be helping granddad and teasing their cousin as usual."

"Betty is great, isn't she?" I commented. "She keeps the family going despite the number of hours Nicholas works and all those business trips. Don't know how she manages."

"Yes, he's a lucky man. She runs the house like clockwork. Nicholas is like his dad: anything for a quiet life, but he works much longer hours than we did in our day."

"Our only trips were on the snow coach." I chuckled. "Do you think they'll have any more children?"

"No. Betty has put her foot down – no more nappies and sleepless nights." Nicola replied. "Andy said they should continue until they have a football team. Betty was not amused!"

"Don't blame her," I agreed. "Three children are enough for anyone. How are they getting on at school?"

"Superstars," beamed the proud grandmother. "All sports crazy and thankfully all support QPR like their dad and Uncle Neil."

The awkward silence preceded the apology from Nicola. "Sorry. You realise Andy has invited Neil and his wife and her children?"

"Andy did not mention it, but he didn't have to – he's Andy's best mate. There're joined at the hip unless they are playing darts." I changed the subject quickly as a distraction from the apprehension I felt facing Neil and his wife. "Okay, party girl – where's your blue eye shadow?"

"In the shop!" Nicola retorted. "I'm not wearing bright eyeshadow – I'll look like a parrot!"

"Yes, and?" I giggled. "What have you done with the shoulder pads?"

"They're in the wardrobe," Nicola groaned. "I haven't got time trying to fiddle with them."

"Won't take me a minute to fix them back and you can take them out when you do the YMCA!" I said trying to keep a straight face.

"You're enjoying this aren't you?" Nicola asked impatiently.

"Yep!" I replied.

"Haven't you gone yet?" Nicola called out.

"Just adjusting my tights," I said. "Need to make sure the glittery heart is showing after the money I spent on them."

"You're sixty; not sixteen," Nicola retorted. "No one is going to notice anything on your legs. You better go soon – you're supposed to be helping Andy with the balloons."

'Balloons?' I mouthed.

"Yes!" Nicola groaned. "Balloons. Andy's nieces want balloons so they can flick them around when they are bored. Sorry, I should say, they can pass them around for fun."

"You're such a moany minny," I chortled. "Come on, get your party head on before I go."

Nicola tried another attempt at the surprise expression.

"Where is Rose?" I asked.

"She'd better get back soon," Nicola's voice wobbled with tension whilst waiting for her daughter to return from work. "Andy's sister will start flustering around if I'm too late."

"Does Rose know it's a "*not*" surprise party?" I asked.

"What do I know?" a gruff voice rattled along the hall.

"Where've you been?" Nicola complained.

"Working!" Rose snapped.

"Wish you'd get a more secure job with more sociable hours," Nicola said.

"What? Like be a secretary and find a nice sweet compliant husband?" Rose retaliated and then the two hot headed females in the family went into battle.

"Well it's better than your ex-husband who quite literally ran off," Nicola's sharpness took me aback. I could only equate it to concern that her daughter risked injury if she continued being a Personal Trainer. Rose married at seventeen, had a child at eighteen, and divorced at nineteen. Her husband pursued his goal to be in the Olympics – there was no time or space in his life for a family. Rose is a rebel but appreciates support from her parents to look after her teenage daughter who is far more relaxed – she takes after her granddad.

"How about fitness classes for OAPs? That would be a bit more stable." Rose retorted. "I will sign you and Mary up – you can even have a special discount!"

I intervened in the crossfire. "I hate to break up this happy family disagreement, but we need to leave soon. What am I doing?"

"Blimey, it's like living in a retirement home!" Rose sounded incredibly disgruntled at the tedious situation and blurted out, "you've got to go to help dad; that is – rescue him from Aunty Jenny! I'm taking mum to the church hall: she thinks there is going to be a charity concert organised by my running club. Everyone understand or do you want me to write it down for you?"

"I'm off, and just a reminder," I teased my fraught friend and her daughter, "it's time for smiley faces."

***

Nicola put on her best surprise face, and it was not too bad. Most people believed her acting skills. Rose winked at me to acknowledge she had succeeded in her mission.

Andy gave his wife a kiss on the cheek which was a rare public display of affection. Nicola blushed but gave her husband a hug not only for organising her party but for thirty-four years of happy marriage – not glamorous but grounded, not loud but loving and not false but forgiving.

Andy's nieces played with the balloons and annoyed their mother, his sister, when they fell on the buffet table – disturbing the arrangement of chicken Vol au Vents and ham sandwiches. The game came to a sharp halt when a yellow balloon burst upon contact with the cocktail stick holding cheese and pineapple pieces. A fine retro food display crowned with an extraordinarily large strawberry trifle balancing precariously too close to the edge of the table, for my liking.

I found a table in the corner, away from the hubbub of the entrance.

"Aunty!" Christine's overexcited voice woke me up from my daydream. "How are you? Love your glitter tights!"

"Really?" I said with a smile. "Did your grandmother tell you to say that?"

"No!" she replied sheepishly. "Well, sort of. But I still think they are dotty."

"*Dotty?*" I thought. "*Best not to ask.*" I gave Nicola and Andy's granddaughter a hug and said, "you must be exhausted, the decorations look wonderful. Did you keep granddad in line?"

"Yes, of course," Christine replied cheekily. "But the gruesome twosome got under our feet! They are such a pain but it's funny to watch when they wind up Great Aunty Jenny."

"Christine, stop being snippy," I said in my best aunty voice even though I am not biologically her aunt and thankful she does not refer to me as a great aunt. She laughed and asked, "what would you like to drink? Can I get you some sandwiches? I would offer the Vol-au-Vents but they're a bit squidgy and dirty after the balloons!"

I watched Christine, a thirteen-year-old going on thirty and wondered how her character could be polar opposite to her mother. Nicola and Andy were tormented by their daughter, Rose, but blessed with their caring granddaughter, Christine.

"Where's my crazy daughter?" Rose asked.

"She's gone to get me a drink," I replied. "She's run off her feet. We need to clone her."

"Don't know about that," Rose's weary voice wobbled as she slumped in the chair. "Could do with a strong black coffee."

"Here you go aunty; gran told me to give you this. White wine spitz?" Is that what it's called?"

Christine's bemused expression brightened when she saw her mother. "Mum, great job getting gran into the party – she looked so surprised! Do you want a prosecco?"

"Thanks, but no. Could you get me a black coffee to go

"Where are you going mum?" an anxious daughter dreaded the usual answer.

"Work, I'm afraid," Rose replied. "No rest for us single mums. Your clothes cost a lot of money."

Christine scuttled off to get the coffee and I felt the need to say, "That's a bit harsh, isn't it? Nicola and Andy pay for most of Christine's clothes. She's a bit young to carry the debt burden guilt trip on her shoulders?"

"Look who's talking about harsh!" Rose snapped.

"Okay, line judge calls deuce," I relinquished using an expression from tennis which was one sport Rose did not despise unlike football which she loathed due to the endless chatter between her dad and brother and her nephews. "Can't you stay for a little longer, for your mum's sake?"

"What, do you really think she'll notice if I'm here?" Rose protested. "And Christine is too busy being spoilt by her grandparents and aunt – miss perfect housewife, Betty."

"Well, if you're in this type of mood, will be better if you left," I retorted. "At least have the decency to hold on until the photos are taken – it won't be much longer."

"Yeah, okay," Rose mumbled. "Sorry, just so tired, it hurts. I'm nearly thirty – what have I done?"

"What, do you mean, beside drive your mum up the wall?" I chortled.

"Line judge calls, 'game set and match to Aunty Mary!" Rose conceded and yawned.

"I thought you're going trekking to Kilimanjaro?" I asked. "That should get you a few likes on your socials."

Rose laughed loudly, "Ooh, look at Aunty Mary keeping up with socials! What next? Your own podcast?"

"Very funny!" I replied. "You really would not want me to interview your mum on my podcast, would you?"

Christine rushed up to the table, "Look mum, Aunty Betty found this recycled carboard cup and lid for a takeaway."

Red hues of frustration filled Rose's face, but she bit her lip. "Thanks. You're a star! Ask gran – when are we going to take the photos?" Christine marched off on another errand for her mother.

"Where would you like to go for your birthday?" I asked.

Rose nodded her head and in a deflated tone said, "Nowhere thanks, can't cope with mum fussing and playing happy families. I'll just go out for a drink or two with mates from the running club."

"Why don't we go to the Victoria and Albert Museum? Just us two? Will be nice to catch up properly." I made the enquiry and was astounded by the answer.

"Sounds great! Could do with a day off."

The photographer, Andy hired, gathered everyone in groups for the various awkward photos in addition to those he took when Nicola arrived. A couple of images were uploaded to Instagram to keep the hungry wolves of social media users at bay, i.e. those who could not attend.

"Right, I need to go now," Rose announced much to her mother's dismay. "Have fun mum. Don't do anything I would do!" Rose returned to get her jacket from the chair next to my perch and said, "have you seen who has just arrived?"

"No," I whispered and blushed.

"Liar!" Rose replied sharply.

"Alright, I might have caught a glimpse," I admitted. "Where is his wife?"

Rose tutted, "don't you keep up with the gossip? Mum must have told you?" She saw the blank look on my face and continued, "Neil and his wife have been on a bit of a rocky road for well over a year. She goes to stay with her so-called cousin – sort of kissing cousin if you get my drift. So, looks like he's all yours for the taking!"

"Don't be silly," I snapped. "I'm not falling under the gossip mill. Someone's got their wires crossed."

"Your loss," Rose teased. "He ain't all that bad. Dad thinks he's the bees' knees! Send me a text message – we'll arrange a day, yeah?" Rose rushed towards the door – trying her best to avoid the "*I haven't seen you for ages!*" moments.

"Where's mum?" Christine asked.

"She's left, I'm afraid," I replied with empathy as I could see the teenage girl yearning to spend time with her mother.

"Oh, okay!" Christine replied. "I'll get you some sandwiches, aunty, and must move that trifle before the gruesome twosome knock it over. Aunty Betty will be furious."

Christine distracted herself with busyness.

"Anyone sitting here?" the familiar voice startled me.

"You gave me a fright," I mumbled.

"Ain't that bad, am I? I had a shower today and even washed my hair."

"Hope you washed that old blue jumper which still doesn't fit you properly," I laughed.

"Fits just fine." Neil Bach's smile broadened and my face glowed. "Oh, by the way, I thought you may like these?" Neil left a small packet of salted peanuts on the table.

"Thanks," I replied softly.

"Can I get you a drink?" Neil asked.

"Yes, please," I replied eagerly. "White wine spritzer!"

The catchy chorus of the song, 'Don't You Want Me' by The Human League, reverberated around the hall; prompting guests to sing along even if they were using the wrong words. No one really minded – it lifted our spirits. Christine nudged her granddad and said, "See: we should have ordered a karaoke machine." Andy laughed loudly and hugged his beloved granddaughter.

The DJ then changed direction and played, 'Only You' by Yazoo.

"Bit early for a slow dance," said Neil. "DJ must be having a break. If he has any of that trifle he'll be out for the night. Can smell the brandy from here!" Neil had not lost his sense of humour and out of the corner of my eye I could see Nicola grin as she saw my face light up. Neil and me made our way to the dance floor for old time's sake. After a few awkward moments readjusting our hand placements, I rested my left hand lightly on his right shoulder and held out my right arm at a strange angle. He gently held my right hand, and the tingling sensation sent a wave of emotion to the depth of my hidden feelings. The tears in my eyes were visible so I reverted to humour for distraction. "Have you had dance lessons?"

"No," Neil replied mischievously, "this is pure natural talent."

"Really?" I quipped.

"I wasn't that bad?" Neil asked.

"I've still got the bruises," I teased and we both laughed and relaxed.

"Better sit down." I said, "my old bones can't take all this exercise."

Andy came to see if Neil wanted a drink and cheekily asked if I needed First Aid. Neil and Andy laughed like naughty school children.

"Very funny," I retorted. "Please can you get me a drink before I melt."

"Are you sure?" Andy asked cheekily. "You need to be careful at your age." Neil could not stifle his laughter. "Okay, you asked for it," I said, "I'm telling Nicola."

"What are you going to tell me?" Nicola intervened. Andy pointed at Neil and Neil pointed at Andy. She continued, "will someone get my dearest old friend a drink before she faints from exhaustion." Andy and Neil scuttled towards the bar.

Nicola sat down and said, "nice to see you smiling – I mean real smiling not the one on the mask you wear."

"Too tired for counselling session," I groaned. Although I relished a few moments recapturing the fun times of the gang I turned to a serious point, "Is Andy concerned about Neil and me?"

"He's very protective of Neil," Nicola replied. "Always has been, but the situation with Caroline has been twisting him in knots. Neil can't take much more pain at the moment, and we all know how fond he is of you. Don't you?"

I stared at my best friend and acknowledged her correct assessment. "Don't know what you mean?" I smiled.

After a few sips of white wine spritzer and another handful of peanuts, I felt re-energised and joined Christine as she danced to the song, 'Come on Eileen' by Dexys Midnight Runners. She did not mind dancing with her honorary great aunty because by this stage in the evening, most guests were too merry to notice. Although she tried her best to avoid the secret video takers using their mobiles. One minute on the dance floor and the next minute trending on twitter or X-files or something like that!

"You've got more energy now than you did all those years ago?" Neil observed from his chair.

"Cheek!" I replied. "Are you going to keep that jumper on all night?"

"Yes, of course. It's my favourite," Neil said as he held his hand to his chest, "holds a lot of memories."

"Surprise it holds together," I quipped. "Talk about recycling."

"Any luck with your flat?" Neil asked tentatively.

"Do we have to talk about sensible boring topics?" I groaned.

"Not at all," Neil said apologetically.

"That's okay," I said wearily. "All a bit of a strain. Wouldn't mind a night off thinking about it, if you don't mind!"

"Don't mind at all and don't blame you," Neil replied. "I've also been on the receiving end of Tarquin's sales pitch– forceful or robotic – not sure which one!"

"A cyber man or a dalek?" I pondered. "Programmed to repeat – we will sell your flat now!" We both laughed which helped ease the stress of moving.

"Is your wife okay?" I asked and immediately regretted the words emanating from my mouth but felt the need to justify the reason for my inappropriate enquiry. "Nicola said you were coming with your family?"

"Originally yes, but she changed her mind. The children, well her children are too old to go to these retro parties."

"Sorry. Didn't you want children of your own?" My face and neck flushed bright red. "Sorry, terrible question – can I take two?"

"No worries," Neil said reassuringly, "people say it all the time or should I say people think of it all the time. Went through a couple of years – thought it'd be nice. She said she couldn't get pregnant – got a bit confused but then found contraceptives in the bathroom. Bit disheartening really, but it's her body and suppose she didn't want to go through all that pain again. So, we carried on – and I took care of the children, but they were fairly independent when I arrived so not much to do. Caroline has a great career – got promotion much easier than me – she's the one with the brains."

"And you've got the beauty!?" I tried to lighten the mood.

"You could say that!" Neil smiled.

The DJ saved me from my extraordinary 'foot in mouth' moment as he played, '*Down Under*' by Men at Work

"Come on," I said, "we've got to dance to this one for Warren's sake. Do you hear from him?"

"Yes." Neil replied, "he has a great life – sun, sea, and sand – lovely family and home. Good old Warren – he stood up for us, didn't he?"

"Sure did!" I replied loudly. We tried to have a conversation on the dance floor – a strange eccentric custom which is as bizarre as dancing around handbags.

Nicola and Andy joined us. "Best dad dancing – EVER!" I squealed excitedly. Neil applauded in agreement, Nicola burst into laughter, and Andy stuck out his tongue. The awesome foursome reunited on the dance floor for a fleeting moment. Worries and fears pushed to one side.

"Ouch!" I complained. "My feet are aching!"

"Take your shoes off!" Neil responded jokingly,

"Do you know how much these shoes cost?" I teased.

"I dread to think," Neil replied. "Bet those are designer and broke the piggy bank?"

"Not quite," I smiled. "Twenty pound in the charity shop. A good bargain but my feet are paying the price for an ill fitted shoe. Vanity is for the young!"

"I can give you a lift if you want?" Neil asked. "I don't need to use a sat nav – I know where you live."

"Aunty, I've got slipper ballerina pumps!" Christine called out. "Haven't got any for you uncle!"

"You're an angel!" I said and gave Christine a big hug, "she's great, isn't she?"

"Sure is?" Neil replied slowly as the tinge of regret slipped past his eyes. In his moment of distraction he asked, "no children for you?" and immediately apologised. "Sorry. Bit too personal?"

"No children," I said. "Not too personal. I know Nicola would tell you if I had kids"

"Not so," Neil responded reassuringly, "she doesn't tell me everything despite what you think. Andy only tells me what Nicola tells him to tell me. If that makes any sense?"

"Not a bit of sense," I laughed, "but applaud you for trying to explain especially at this time at night!"

"You old timer," Neil teased. "It's early doors – party is just warming up!"

"I'm worn out!" I said.

"I'll just go to the little boys' room, and I'll give you a lift. Okay?"

I nodded in agreement. Just as Neil returned, the song, 'It Must Be Love' by Madness started.

"There're playing our song!" Neil beamed with delight. "Should we dance?"

"Rude not too," I smiled.

***

"Well, well?" Nicola shouted down the phone.

"Well, what?" I yawned repeatedly.

"Did Neil go for a private viewing?"

"No, absolutely no!" "What was I supposed to do, offer him coffee amongst the packing boxes?"

"You've nothing to hide – he's seen the place already! You might have got a good deal if he wanted a quick sale!"

"Have you been on that trifle?" I asked.

"No! Andy finished that last night hence why he is still in the bathroom."

"Too much detail! What has gotten into you?" My question did not deter the probe for details.

"Sooo happy to see you with Neil again." Nicola purred with delight.

"Two golden oldies trying to dance to records from the 80's and complaining about our aches and pains. And can you believe he's still got that jumper? How is that possible?" I asked.

"He kept it wrapped up in the back of the wardrobe!"

"How do you know that?" My question led to an interesting insight.

"He told Andy." Nicola responded.

"Blimey, didn't think blokes talk about knitwear on the football terraces?" I chortled.

"You're such a grouch!" When are you going to see him again?" Nicola enquired.

"Tarquin says there's another viewing next week or during the week – it's all noise – have to block it out otherwise I'll go round the bend." I replied wearily.

"So, that's it? You're a seller and he's a potential buyer?"

"Yes. What did you expect to happen?" I retorted.

"At least go out for pie and chips or game of darts"

"Are you still drunk?" The sarcasm in my voice prompted a sharp response.

"No. Are you still frumpy?"

"Yes, absolutely; grumpy frumpy and exhausted," I said. "Going to have forty winks and then contact Rose about our trip to the Victoria and Albert Museum."

"Good luck getting a reply." Nicola groaned under the weight of dismay at the distance of her daughter.

"She'll reply to her favourite aunty!" I giggled.

***

CHAPTER 11

"Won't be a minute!" Susie Beatty, the loyal family hairdresser, called out from behind the reception desk.

"That's fine – fully understand," I replied.

"Right!" Susie said, "sorry about all that. Roshni got her days mixed up; so just squeezed her in for a cut and blow dry. Poor thing, she is run off her feet!"

"Roshni? Sunil's wife?" I enquired.

"Yes. Sunil's health is declining but they're determined to keep the Newsagents open until they look into all the options about renting the shop or refurbishing the entire building."

"I feel so sorry for them," I said. "Do you think their sons will take over?"

"No," Susie replied. "They're far too happy and wealthy in their careers as techie specialists but they do not want the Estate Agents putting more pressure on them to sell."

"You mean Tarquin?" I groaned.

"Now you come to mention it," Susie chortled. "On the topic of Tarquin."

I intervened, "do we have to?"

Susie laughed, "I know exactly what you mean. He was in last week for a quick, tidy up, as he calls it."

"Was he moaning about me?" I fished for feedback.

"Not really," Susie stuttered and then said directly, "yes! He said you've had loads of offers for your flat and you haven't made up your mind? He drives me to distraction but give him his due he does provide free advertising by recommending my shop."

"I don't think two offers equates to '*loads*' but in Tarquin's universe, anything is possible," I quipped. "I need time to think and look around more properties."

"Hence the haircut," Susie enquired, "you want to impress the current owners of your new home. You know what they say, first impression is the last impression!"

"Yes, that's true," I acknowledged her astute observation. "But also want to get ready for Edie's visit."

"Oh, how lovely!" Susie shrilled. "When will Edie be here? Back together again – like it should be."

"She's arriving Thursday," I replied. "Staying or should I say squashing into my flat for the weekend and then going to stay with Sebastian for his birthday."

"Fantastic!" Susie yelped. "How old is Sebastian?"

"Forty-two on Tuesday," I sighed, "where do the years go?"

"If you ever find out, please let me know," Susie laughed and then asked the '*elephant in the room*' question. "How old is Domenico?"

"Forty-seven," I replied and reassured our family friend, "it's okay, everyone asks or wants to ask the same question. Domenico is more mature than he looks, and the beauty is that he is so comfortable in his own skin – so relaxed. He is not in competition with anyone – does not need to be."

"I agree he is absolutely beautiful!" Susie giggled like a schoolgirl which was nice to hear because she was under similar pressure to other business owners in an ever-changing High Street.

"Yes, extremely handsome," I said, " and extremely loyal. I couldn't be happier for her."

"Must be a slight bit of jealousy creeping in now and then?" Susie teased.

"Okay, just a smidgen," I conceded.

"Never mind," said Susie in an uplifting tone, "you're on your way to finding Mr Right, especially with those new nails. You really are pushing the boat out! I'll have to up my game to match the colours and style."

***

"Mind the box!" My warning signal went unheeded.

Edie tripped and hit her arm against the bedroom door frame and gave out a loud, "OW!!"

"Tried to warn you," I said smugly.

"No need to rub it in," Edie moaned. "Where shall I put my case?"

"Wherever you can find a space," I replied. "Do you want a tea?"

"Yes, please! I think the taxi driver used to be in Wacky Races?" Edie said as she opened the zip of her suitcase and tugged at items of clothing. She hit her elbow against the headboard which restricted the rapidly decreasing space in my bedroom.

"Wacky Races?" I laughed. "That really is a blast from the past. I liked Penelope Pitstop."

"The taxi driver was more like Dick Dastardly without the dog!" Edie said.

"Muttley!" I called out.

"Who!?!" Edie asked. The irritation in her voice was driven by exhaustion following the delayed flight from Florence.

"I'll explain another time when you can keep your eyes open," I said. "Do you want anything to eat?"

"Not really but best if I did," Edie replied. "Promised Domenico I'd eat healthy food but then again he does not know you that well."

"How rude!" I chortled. "There are plenty of healthy options in my cupboard: Weetabix, fruit bread, cereal bars, honey and even porridge!"

"Weetabix please," Edie's request was followed up with a special culinary choice, "is hot milk on the menu. It's much colder here compared to home."

A sense of sadness mixed with relief filled my mind as Edie referred to Florence as home.

Edie's eyelids flickered as she nodded off. She nearly dropped the tray on her lap. Thankfully, her bowl was empty. "Where am I?" She looked startled and then said, "oh, it's you!"

"Love you too," I quipped. "Come on sleepy head, time for bed. And don't worry we're not sharing; I sleep much better in the cosy chair, and I still have the bruises from the last time I shared a bed with you. You're like a horse galloping on the racetrack!"

"If you say so," Edie yawned. "Far too tired to argue."

***

The rattle on the bathroom door woke me up and I called out, "Is that you Edie?"

"No!" She replied, "it's your friendly neighbourhood burglar – just having a comfort break."

"You're back on form!" I quipped.

"Yes," Edie replied, "and raring to go – finish packing these boxes. Talk about health and safety!"

I ignored her critique and said, "it's your turn to make the tea. And toast and jam will be lovely. Thank you." The muttering and grumbling drifted to the living room. I laughed at the surreal set of circumstances and thought, *'Our lives have turned on their head within the last few years, but we can still find time to grumble about domestic chores.'*

The rattling on my mobile disturbed my pensive mood. Tarquin's voice boomed through the handset, "Mary. Good morning! How are you?"

"Well, thank you," I replied suspiciously.

"Good! Good!" He proclaimed insincerely and continued, "potential buyers with me now. Can we pop around for 10 minutes?"

"NO!" I replied forcibly. Maybe too forcibly bearing in mind my circumstances. I did not need Tarquin but needed help to move in some shape or format. "Sorry," I apologised reluctantly but thought it was a wise option. I continued explaining and knew deep down Tarquin was not listening but persisted, "we agreed during the week, and I sent an e-mail to Quenton to confirm there are no viewings until after Tuesday 14th."

"But we'll only stick our heads around the door," Tarquin put the pressure on. "You won't notice we're there."

"You're right, I won't notice, because no one is coming here," I snapped. "I have personal commitments. This is an important weekend and so is Tuesday." Tarquin did not take the bait about his eldest son's birthday. There was not even a flicker of recognition of the date – it meant nothing to him beside another day to seal the deal: my brain has been infiltrated with his nonsensical catch phrases.

"Your loss," Tarquin ended the call abruptly.

"Who was that?" Edie enquired.

"I give you three guesses," I replied.

"Oh! No one important then," Edie chuckled. "I thought it might have been your new boyfriend?"

"Boyfriend!?!" I retorted and nearly dropped my toast.

"Well, don't be shy," my sister teased. "Can't remember the last time you wore nail varnish, and you've got new highlights. And even more shockingly did I see gym clothes in your washing basket?"

"You're so nosey!" I complained.

"No, just curious," Edie said as she observed my reddened face and looked at me with a sideway glance.

"There's no boyfriend," I said, "and not exactly the ideal time to meet someone. Never mind saying, I haven't got anything to wear; I can't find anything to wear, beside jeans and tee-shirt."

"I believe you," Edie chortled, "many wouldn't. In fact, I'm still not sure – call it woman's instinct."

"Ask Jo," I set out my weak defence, "she'll tell you."

"Tell me?" Edie laughed. "She doesn't pick up my calls unless she needs something."

"That's mean," I said. "Ask her when you see her."

Edie, although usually feisty, looked serious and sad. "She's too busy working! Not even coming to the meal for Sebastian's birthday."

"She's probably going to help with auditions again." I tried to provide an explanation, but it came across as a feeble excuse.

"Auditions for what? The next Prime Minister?" Edie snapped.

"She'll call you," I tried to reassure my sister – a mother racked with guilt for moving abroad conflicted with a woman who had found the unique and highly unusual mutually respective relationship.

"She's still angry with me?" Edie asked and almost answered at the same time.

"Yep!" My answer was brutal but felt there was no point in beating around the bush any longer. Everyone knew

Jo resented her mother leaving Kent but were too reluctant to verbalise the obvious situation

"What am I supposed to do?" Edie growled. "I can't turn the clocks back and I'm not leaving Domenico for a petulant child who can't be bothered to see her mother for an hour!"

I cannot recall the last time, if at all, I heard such vitriol from Edie's mouth. I put it down to jetlag which made no sense at all because Florence is only one hour ahead of Greenwich Mean Time and then began to worry if she had hit a wobbly patch in her relationship. I asked the dreaded questions, "How is Domenico? Are things all right with you two?"

"Fantastico!" Edie's tone relaxed immediately at the mention of her second husband. "He's looking after his mother; she sprained her wrist last week after a fall and he wants to make sure she rests, and he can treat her to his delicious cooking." The happiness in her voice and displayed on her face reassured me and was so thankful this level of peace came knocking at her door and she opened herself up to accept this blessing. Jo would not use the word blessing however I hold onto the hope that Jo will accept and respect that her mother is free from Tarquin's torment. Another matter that could explain Edie's level of stress was being in proximity to her ex-husband. I told her there were no viewings during her stay. Of course, Tarquin had to telephone, and it would not surprise me if he turned up at the door. Someone is providing him with information. A little niggle at the back of my mind tells me it is Jo but try to blot that accusation out of my psyche in an attempt to retain some form of equilibrium in my mind.

"Has Domenico called?" I asked.

"He doesn't need to," Edie replied. When she saw my confused expression she explained, "he trusts me and is comfortable and respectful to enable me to spend quality time with my family."

"Is he human?" I laughed. "There must be one annoying habit?"

The tension on Edie's face eased and she said, "He's not keen on ironing but I can live with that – just about!"

"Oh, you poor thing!" I teased.

"Which boxes do you want me to start on now?" Edie asked eagerly.

"None," I replied wearily. "Tools down! Time for a break. I'm treating you to lunch at one of the finest restaurants on the High Street."

"Should I put on my best dress?" Edie asked mockingly.

"Not quite," I said sheepishly. "We're going to the Wimpy restaurant."

"Seriously?!" Edie exclaimed. "There's no expense spared with you is there?"

"Thought we could say goodbye to Reg before he retires," I said. "Poor man is exhausted, and Elsie is at breaking point. They're finalising legal documents and going to Spain – they can hardly wait.

"What's happened to their children?" Edie asked.

"The twin boys emigrated to Australia and their sisters moved to Scotland. They hardly see or hear from them. Don't think Elsie or the family recovered after her long stays in the convalescent home in Tunbridge Wells. She had so many health problems after the twins were born and then she had a break down, allegedly. No one really talked about it then."

"Poor woman," Edie sighed. "Didn't know all that happened. What is Reg's middle name? Remember mum saying his mother was French? How did that work out? He's from the East End, isn't he?"

"Reg Béchu Rees," I announced proudly because I remembered how dad explained the story about Reg's parents. "His father was an East End boy, but no one could find out how he met a creative French woman – excellent at needlecraft and a devoted wife even though her husband had a wandering eye. She doted on Reg – their only child. Legend has it that Reg has half brothers and sisters, but they do not keep in touch – not keen on the link to a fast-food shop. Remember mum telling me that the name Béchu means *'one who talks a lot'*."

"You're doing enough talking for all of us," Edie complained. "Jo would be furious about you babbling on about the meaning of names again."

"I'm not babbling, just reminiscing about the good old days," I chirped.

"They weren't all good!" Edie frowned.

"No, they weren't but the High Street had a completely different feel and at least the neighbours knew each other and more importantly, helped each other. Really not comfortable living around here anymore."

"Well, move then, silly!" Edie gave her order with gusto and then gave an announcement of her lunch order. "Come on, there is a cheeseburger with lots of onions with my name on it."

We both laughed with echoes of our childhood following us along the shared corridor and down the stairs to the main entrance.

***

The days with Edie flew by. We squabbled like children, ate too much cake, and squandered time on binge watching vintage TV: from dramas such as Upstairs Downstairs and

The Professionals; to classic comedy shows e.g. Dinner Ladies, As Time Goes By, and To the Manor Born. With a few moments fitted in for the original cartoon versions of Tom & Jerry and Bugs Bunny.

We reflected and recalled our time with dad when we watched The Festival of Remembrance at The Royal Albert Hall on the Saturday evening, and the service at The Cenotaph on Remembrance Sunday. We only went through two boxes of tissues – so not bad by my standards.

I was torn whether to drop into the conversation the surreal circumstances in relation to Neil Bach. In the end I decided not to, or should I say, avoided the issue. Filled with confusion and mixed emotions, I put the subject in the pending folder in my wardrobe and focused on the shared moments with my older sister who I miss immensely.

Edie went to her son's home on Tuesday 14th November to celebrate his birthday and spend time with her grandchildren. Still hard to think of my sister as a grandmother especially as she now looks ten years younger than me. The lifestyle in Florence appears to be the best spa for health and wellbeing.

***

CHAPTER 12

"Jo, if you don't return my calls, I'm going to phone Georgios directly! Don't worry I'll find his number." I threw my mobile on the bed which fell off the other side and slid under the wardrobe.

"BOOP!" I exclaimed. "That's not meant to happen." After I finished thinking aloud, I started the operative procedure of retrieving my mobile from the dusty cobwebs lurking under the wardrobe.

By the time I reached the mobile there were two missed calls and an irate voicemail message from Jo: "If you want me to talk to you – might help if you answer your mobile!"

"Hello," I said sweetly, "how is my favourite niece?"

"Only niece!" Jo retorted. "What do you want?"

"To ask how you are?" My enquiry about Jo's wellbeing was met with the box standard reply.

"Busy!" Jo snapped.

"Too busy to call your mother?" I asked.

"Far too busy to call anyone," Jo tutted and made the statement, "I'll call on Monday – if I get a break during the afternoon. By the time we finish at night she's fast asleep. Don't need to worry about waking up Domenica, he doesn't sleep – he's a robot – no man can be that perfect!"

"Oh my! Oh my!" I teased. "The Green-Eyed Monster is getting stronger and bigger. How can a 35-year-old be jealous of their mother?"

"Easy!" Jo retorted, "have you seen where she lives? And I live in a grotty bed sit in dirty London."

"Better living in London than spending hours commuting," I said sternly but conceded – there was absolutely no point getting entangled in a dispute with Jo when she was hiding behind such a thick defensive wall."

"Yeah. Whatever!" Jo groaned. "Need to go soon. I'll pop around to see you tomorrow?"

"I'm afraid I have a date," I replied sniggering, knowing all too well Jo would bite back.

"Date?" Jo squealed. "Who with, the removal man?"

"Very funny," I said. "Nicola's taking me out for Christmas drinks. There's a new cocktail bar near Elmar Park station, and they have a Salsa Night.

"You sure, you'll get in?" Jo quipped.

"Don't think they'll ask for our ID, but I'll bring it just in case," I teased.

"Can we pencil in a date, actually near Christmas, not on 1st December?" Jo enquired.

"Nicola is really busy before Christmas, so this is the best date," I said. "There's a Carol Service in St. John's next Thursday. You're welcome to come along. Nicola is making the mince pies and Sebastian and Sophia are going with the children."

"No, can't," Jo replied despondently. "We've got more auditions and promised I'd help with the arrangements."

"Never mind," I said with equal regret. "If things change, there'll be a seat for you, or you might have to stand based on the response so far. Dale Estate Agents are sponsoring the catering and drinks. Your dad has been promoting the event at every opportunity as you can imagine – showing how they are supporting the Community. He's promising mulled wine, Christmas cake, chocolates, and satsumas for the healthy option."

"More like, propaganda on their website!" Jo protested. "They have to pretend to care about the elderly even though they really want to get their hands on their property to sell at an enormous profit. Commission comes before Christianity."

I was confused by Jo's defence of Christianity, but it was motivated by anger directed at her father.

"Why hasn't he sold your flat?" Jo fumed. "He could sell a selfie to The National Gallery."

"Not sure what to do for the best?" I replied feebly and asked, "I assume you are referring to your dad?"

"Yes, of course, who else has such a brash selling technique but surprised he hasn't bullied you into selling. Surely someone must be interested?"

"Yes." I hesitated. "Someone I used to know many years ago. I am not making it up – such a surreal set of circumstances. At least the flat would be in a safe pair of hands, but do not know what to say to him? Tarquin over inflates each word, so we are just going around in circles."

"Easy," Jo replied. "ChatGPT dude!"

"Where is that line from," I asked naively.

"Just a line from a risqué comedy series on TV – you've never watched it!" Jo mocked.

"Try me!" I prodded proactively. "You never know – does it have the woman with blue hair?"

I could almost hear Joanna rolling her eyes. "How out of touch are you? Really!? Never mind – will explain another time when we have a few hours to waste! Note to myself – I never want to get old."

"Soz," I chortled. "Can't stop getting old."!

Joanna tutted in disgust, "there is nothing worse than an oldie trying to be young! Soz!?! Where did you dig that up from?" Jo made a hurried exit by giving the excuse someone was calling her.

We made a tentative agreement to meet one week before Christmas. In the interim my focus on decluttering, recycling, and donating to Charity shops escalated at pace. I made excuses not to have any more viewings for one week – the more noise from Tarquin created more distraction from decisive action. Nicola, no doubt, will read the riot act to me tomorrow evening. Funny how we used to call it a 'girls' night out' – seems only yesterday. Now it is two mature ladies chatting about changes and consequences. It could be our last chance to go out for an evening for quite a while if I move to Italy. Jo keeps reminding me of the reality check: it is only a short flight to Italy. I do not need to book a ticket on a space rocket not that I could afford their prices even with an old age pensioner pass.

The social Salsa evening might not be the wisest idea; I could end up in Accident & Emergency which is the last thing I need when maybe moving. But it will be an opportunity for Nicola and me to let our hair down and de-stress; dance as if no one is watching. In the good old days Andy and Neil would join in dancing after a few pints. Even in their younger years they were experts at dad dancing. I sense Andy is growing increasingly concerned about Neil and is not keen on him reopening old wounds. Andy tends to blame me, in a passive aggressive way, for the breakdown of the relationship between Neil and me. As a group of four friends we were a good team in corporate language but on a more emotional level, a closely knitted support for each other. The edges started to fray, and I dropped the stitch holding us together. Neil was most certainly the one that got away, and I did not realise how much I lost until now. The dilemma is: do I risk entering a relationship albeit a friendship initially – I have learnt that lesson the hard way.

Or do I pack up, emigrate, and immerse myself in a new chapter?

***

CHAPTER 13

My niece, Joanna Tabitha Crowmere-Gale, stomped into the living room and complained as she knocked into the high stack of packing boxes. Her grumbling came to an abrupt halt, and she said, "Oh, how cosy; aren't you going to introduce me?"

My face reddened with embarrassment mixed with annoyance at the disruption. "Jo, this is a potential buyer."

"Does potential buyer have a name or is he an agent for a secret buyer?" Jo quipped.

"Please excuse my niece," I said condescendingly, "she sometimes forgets to put her manners in her handbag. Okay, let's start again. Take two as they say in Theatreland. Jo, this is Neil. And Neil, may I introduce you to my niece, who I love dearly even though she winds me up for a hobby."

Neil's smile broadened and his eyes glistened as he looked at me. He always found it amusing when I became agitated. He said my face brightened and looked more beautiful.

"Nice to meet you." Neil said and held out his hand, but Jo did not reciprocate the friendly greeting.

"You can tell; my niece is not a diplomat. The Ice Queen will melt eventually." My niece tutted and rolled her eyes in embarrassment and disgust.

"It's fine," Neil said. "Fully understand. Suppose you don't remember me? No, you were only a baby."

"Quite a cute baby in all senses of the word," I teased. "Is it time to get out the embarrassing photos – found some real corkers when going through my albums."

"Don't you dare!" Jo snapped and stared at me with laser sharp precision.

"Spoilsport. It's an aunty's prerogative, in fact her duty, to share the most embarrassing photos!"

My niece's stone-cold facial expression eased when she fired questions towards Neil, "Sorry. What did you say? When did you meet me as a child? Were you a friend of Tarquin's?"

I intervened, "she means her dad." My niece moaned and shook her head as if to say, "stop interrupting!"

Neil explained, "no. I was a friend of your aunt."

"You mean boyfriend?" Jo snapped. "No need to be shy with me. We don't have any secrets do we aunty?"

"No sweetie." I replied. "Only things you think are secret but your mum and me know already! Can't fool your old aunty."

My niece retaliated, "want a bet?"

Neil started to become slightly uncomfortable with the heightened emotions and brash banter. He announced, "We better leave soon. Table is booked for 1 p.m."

"Yeah," Jo responded sharply, "table for me and aunty."

I intervened hesitantly, "Neil has offered to take us to lunch – that'll be okay?"

Jo responded dishearteningly, "know what they say? Two's company, three's a crowd."

"I'll be the nominated gooseberry." Neil tried to ease the awkwardness hanging in the air.

"You said it!" Jo quipped.

"But you were thinking it!" I interjected. "Neil's paying – including cocktails. Only hope you've got your American Express black card." I smiled at Neil.

"Am afraid I left it at home," he laughed. "Only joking – I wouldn't qualify for one of those."

"You can cross him off your list, aunty!" Jo smirked.

I pushed my niece into the hall and muttered, "just stop! He's a good friend and he could really help if he buys the flat."

"What, for you and him or is it going to be his play den?" Jo muttered. "Assume he's married or is he wearing a ring for fun?"

"Okay," I pointed out firmly. "One more chance or you'll be getting a sandwich at the station!"

Lunch was a mixture of delicious food, colourful cocktails, and awkward small talk. My niece was quite restrained and subdued. I asked her, "you staying over? We could go shopping tomorrow. You remember? Real shops with real people!"

"Ha! Ha!" Jo replied. "Very funny. Yeah, be good – need a new pair of jeans, but don't want to get in the way."

"You're not in the way," I replied. "I'll sleep on the settee as usual. We can't have Princess hurting her back."

"You can't both fit on the settee," Jo's provocative comment caused a red hue to rise on my face.

"Don't be silly!" I replied irritably. "He's not sleeping in my flat. Sorry. Neil's not staying overnight in my home tonight or any night."

"Stop digging aunty!" Jo chortled. "Far too cringeworthy."

Neil blushed profusely and called for the bill.

Jo acknowledged his willingness to pay for the lunch and said, "thanks. Just going outside for a cigarette. Do you smoke?"

"No, not now, "Neil replied. "Still remember when Mary, sorry, your aunt, and me used to smoke in the office. How times change."

"Really?" Jo responded sarcastically. "How interesting."

"I'll meet you outside," I said. "If you're a good girl, we can go to the charity shops on the way home." Jo grunted and left the restaurant.

"Boy, she's a feisty character but she's got a great sharp sense of humour," Neil's observation about his challenging lunch guest hit the nail on the head.

"Sharp is an accurate description," I reaffirmed his assessment. "It's a defence mechanism. She has been through some unpleasant experiences. Her dad's attitude does not help."

"Did she say Tarquin?" Neil asked. "Not The Tarquin?" Neil's skill at imitating characteristics and accents had not diminished over the years as he said, "I'm top sales agent of the month."

"Am afraid so!" I replied. "There can only be one Tarquin. He moved up and out of the area for many years but has fallen down to earth with an almighty bump. His company merged – meaning it was taken over by Dale Estate Agents and his prestigious position became a passing phase. So, he's back on his old stomping ground. He's got more contacts here but can't be bothered to contact his children. Better for them really but never nice when your dad ignores you. Jo misses her granddad more than she is letting on. Sorry. I'm rambling on. You best be going. Your wife, oops, mean Caroline, will wonder where you are?"

Neil looked down and melancholy. He said softly, "No. She won't. She has her own life and is spending the week with her cousin – who we know is not really her cousin, but it sounds better for the children and other relatives." He paused and took a deep breath before asking, "can we meet again?"

"Yes. That'll be nice," I replied.

Neil reached out to touch my hand gently. The affectionate gesture did not feel overtly flirtatious nor controlling.

"Reminds me of when we used to sit opposite each other in the staff canteen," he laughed.

"Over a plate of chips and a bit of salad?" I recalled with fondness our simple but special lunches – plain food but precious moments together when we blocked out the surroundings and gaggle of gossipmongers.

"A yoghurt for dessert if we were lucky." Neil smiled. "How romantic!"

A bout of reality shook me back to the present and I coughed in an attempt to cover my embarrassment, and unrelenting yearning to relive that part of my life.

"Is everything okay?" the waiter asked. "Can I get you anything before you leave? Would you like a glass of water?"

"No thank you," Neil replied, "we had a lovely lunch and will certainly be putting a 5-star review on Trip Advisor."

"Thank you, Sir and Madam," the waiter glowed with delight in recognition of his service. "We look forward to seeing you again soon."

I whispered, "I think that is a subtle hint to go."

The cloudless sky sparkled and distracted us from the seasonal freezing temperature. Shoppers bustled along the High Street in a bid to purchase and plan their Christmas celebration which was fast approaching. Five more full days before the festivities begin.

"I'll call Tarquin," Neil said, "tell him I'm still interested and will make an appointment for another viewing if acceptable to the owner?"

"Yes." I smiled and made direct eye contact. "It is acceptable to the owner." I laughed hesitantly and broke the compelling chemistry with a jovial remark, "you better call Super Salesman today otherwise he'll blow a gasket!"

***

The small silver Christmas tree did not look too bad perched on top of the television stand in the corner of my living room taken over by moving boxes and plastic containers. The cards were concertinaed on the other side of the television by the balcony window. Sebastian's kind offer to pick me up on Christmas day, so I could spend time at his home, was welcome and accepted.

In the interim, one cosy chair and heavy box as a temporary footstall – what more did I want? A myriad of thoughts went through my mind. Why do memories keep haunting me? "Because you let them," Jo repeatedly reminds me.

The name of the caller lit up on the screen of my mobile and I winced. The bellowing tones of Tarquin echoed around the room. I pressed the speaker phone option to protect my ears. "Good morning, good morning! How are you, Mary?"

"Good," I replied – self-conscious of how many times we could use the word good between us.

"Good. Good." Tarquin charged forward with his sales pitch. "Listen, good news! We have a private Landlord who wants to expand his portfolio in the area. He's offering way over the market price and will outbid any potential buyer. He has professional tenants queuing up to pay market rent."

"You mean extortionate rent?" I quipped.

"Mary." Tarquin said condescendingly, "it's supply and demand, surely even you know that. You are being offered top dollar for your flat which we can both agree is tired – needs refurbishment which will cost you thousands if you decide to stay."

"Okay," I said reluctantly. "I'll think about it. When does he need an answer?"

"4 p.m. sharp," Tarquin emphasised the exact time loudly.

"What? Today?" I asked.

"Yes, today," Tarquin reiterated his point with impatience. "These deals don't come along every day. He is one of the top clients in South London – he expects results and does not like waiting."

"I will call you back," I said.

"When?" The over hyped Tarquin demanded a precise reply. He became even more frustrated at my reluctance to seal the deal.

"Today," I snapped and ended the call, and put my mobile on silent.

My head thumped and my heart ached. "Oh, why aren't you here dad?" I called out and cried.

"You can't miss out on that offer!" Edie yelled down the phone. "Don't cut your nose off to spite your face!"

"I thought it was too much to expect," I said, "for us to have a calm rational conversation about the sale of the flat."

"Sorry," Edie lowered the volume and continued, "imagine if we lived near each other – days out in Rome or Venice or Florence. Well, our trips will have to be longer than days, but you know what I mean – weekends. The world is our oyster."

"Oysters!" I squirmed. "Yukk!!"

"Fussy boots!" Edie laughed. "Ice-cream then?"

"Okay, you've got yourself a deal." The words slipped out of my mouth, but the enormity of the decision was filled with layers of emotion, pragmatism, and regret.

I thought it was only fair to contact my niece before speaking to Tarquin again. Her response was surprising and entertaining in equal measure. "You're not going to Mars," Jo said. "He can get a flight to Italy. You've missed too much time with mum."

"Are you feeling alright," I asked.

"Absolutely," Jo confirmed. "Anyway – free holidays for me. It's a win-win!"

Nicola's reaction was more pragmatic and poignant with a topping of humour. "Take the money and run. Don't dither. We can't bring back old times, but we can share new times. Imagine having the space to enjoy your life in the sunshine. Andy says there are good football teams in Italy, and you know he likes to go to the games with his best mate. Oh yes, I don't care what Jo says, I am top of the guest list!"

***

The popping of the bottle of champagne raised howls of laughter from the team in Dale Estate Agents. Tarquin thrived on the attention from his colleagues and the members of the public looking through the windows. He shouted, "biggest and best deal of 2023. Back on top where I belong!"

Quenton Seal, the manager, closed the door to his office and picked up the call. "I am sorry Mr Bach; you have been outbid. One of Tarquin's contacts is buying a swathe of property in the area. So, as you can imagine, he's a little busy boasting of his success to the team."

"I can just imagine," Neil replied.

"If you do not mind me saying, Mr Bach, I do not think your heart was really into buying the flat?"

Neil acknowledged the manager's acute perception and said, "No. Not really. The location and timing were not compatible."

***

www.ingramcontent.com/pod-product-compliance
Lightning Source LLC
Chambersburg PA
CBHW051245250626
47155CB00009B/3173